HEARTLESS

BRUTAL ACADEMY

BOOK 1

MAGGIE ALABASTER

JO BRADLEY

CHAPTER 1

HUNTER

I stalked slowly around the table, hands clasped behind my back.

Every so often, I glanced at our 'guest.' That's a term I use loosely, given he was tied to the chair by his ankles and wrists. His mouth was covered with a ragged slash of duct tape.

He was blindfolded with one of his cheap polyester ties when we brought him here. Parker slipped it off so we could see his fear.

Besides, it was easier to get our point across if he could see our faces and the level of shit he was in right now.

He screamed something into the tape and fought against his bindings. His movement rattled the chair. The feet scraped across the concrete floor, screeching painfully.

Parker shook his head. "Scott, Scott, Scott. There's no need to panic. All Hunter and I wanted to do was have a little chat."

Scott eyed him carefully, pain in his gaze. Maybe even a hint of anticipation.

Considering I already removed three of his toes with pruning shears, panic seemed like a good reaction to me. Presumably he was hopeful of getting out of here alive, before he bled out all over the floor.

I tossed one of his toes down onto the table. It bounced a couple of times before it stopped on the edge, right in front of him.

His eyes widened.

"There's a few more where that came from," I reminded him.

He struggled again. Screamed into the tape.

"He knows what he did wrong, doesn't he, Park?" I asked my identical twin brother. "Did we explain it clearly enough?"

Parker sat back in his chair and placed his hands behind his head. "I don't know if we did, Hunt. I suppose he's wondering why he's here."

Scott gave us both a wary look and pressed himself against the back of the chair. As if somehow he could get away from us like that.

"Would you like to explain, or will I?" I asked.

Parker waved his hand at me. "Be my guest."

I raised the pruning shears and slammed them, blades first, into the table. They embedded a centimetre or two, the handle wobbling from the impact.

Scott flinched and jerked away.

I closed my palms down on the table to either side of the shears and leaned forward.

"You may have been ignorant of the fact that Lila Bell belongs to us." I raised an eyebrow at him.

Scott shook his head.

"You didn't know?" I asked.

He nodded.

My other eyebrow joined the first. "You *did* know?" I knew he knew, but fucking with him was too much fun to resist.

His eyes were wide, unsure what to do now.

I straightened up and sat on the edge of the table. "Let's save us both some time. You did know. You knew when you shoved her out of the way in the corridor. You knew when you almost knocked her off her feet. When you knocked books out of her arms."

I leaned forward until I was almost nose to nose with him. He smelled like terror. I inhaled deeply. Scaring the shit out of people was one of the simple joys of life. Particularly when we had good reason to do it.

Scott shook his head and said something against the tape.

I looked over to Parker and nodded. I sat back as my brother ripped the tape off Scott's mouth.

Scott cried out. "I swear to God, it was an accident. I was on my way to class. I was late. Mr D said if I was late again, he'd make sure they'd kick my ass out of Brutham. I can't afford to—"

I slapped my hand down on the table so hard it made Scott and Parker both jump.

"I don't give a fuck if he threatened to kick you out of a fucking aeroplane," I snarled. "You don't touch our woman, and you sure as fuck don't shove her out of the way."

By the sound of it, we were doing Dane DiMarco a favour by dealing with this asshole.

"Man, I'm sorry. I swear, it will never happen again." He pleaded with us both with his eyes. "I was in a hurry and didn't see her. That's all. I sure as fuck didn't mean to—"

"But you did," I said. "At Brutal Academy, running into another guy's woman can get you dead. Any guy. But Lila isn't any guy's woman. She's *our* woman and will be head of the Bell family someday. That's a dangerous fucking combination to make an enemy of, Scott," I told him.

He looked like he wanted to contradict what I

said about Lila leading her family. Chloe, her non-identical twin, was the older sister. If Parker and I had our way, Lila would be the one taking on that role when Samuel Bell stepped down or died. Or, more likely given our lifestyle, was killed.

Life expectancy when you work for criminal organisations, such as our families, was like the shears, short and sharp.

The Bell family and ours were bitter enemies, but Parker, Lila and I would change that. Preferably before her father found out we were fucking her. Our life expectancy would be much shorter than the shears then.

"I swear, I'll look where I am going from now on," Scott whined. "I've learned my lesson. I'll apologise to her again. I'll… I'll do anything, just please…"

His eyes were so wide, I was sure he was about to piss in his jeans. Or shit in them.

Either of those things would make this pleasant chat much less pleasant. I hated when people lost control to that extent. No matter how scared a guy gets, he should be able to control his bodily func-tions. Unless we're talking about his cock. Some of us just get off on fear, ours or someone else's.

Granted, I preferred other people's fear to my own, but I take no responsibility if my cock gets hard, no matter what the circumstances. He has a mind of his own. In fact, he was quite enjoying this. If it wasn't for the smell of sweat and fear, I might insist Scott blow me off. On the other hand, he touched our woman, so he didn't get to enjoy the feeling of my cock in his mouth. That privilege was reserved for people better than him.

"What do you think, Park?" I asked my twin. I was the older and better looking one of us, and the most ruthless. Parker had a way of making people like him, usually right before they found out it was a bad idea to turn their back on him.

"I don't know, Hunt," Parker said slowly. "He seems genuinely sorry for what he did."

"People usually are when they're tied up and missing a couple of toes," I mused. "It tends to make people say things they don't really mean. If we let him walk out of here, he might just go and knock over someone else's woman."

"I won't, I swear," Scott pleaded. "I'll be more careful."

"What do you think Mr D would do if Scotty here shoved his woman out of the way?" I asked thoughtfully.

That begged the question, how many people knew Brutham Academy's history teacher was fucking Chloe Bell, Lila's older sister?

"He'd be pissed," Parker said. "Without doubt,

6

he'd make sure you'd be kicked out of Brutham. Kicked so far no other university in Australia would touch you. Maybe anywhere in the world."

As a DiMarco, Dane probably didn't have that much influence, but Parker got his point across.

"The question is, what does a pair of Brantley brothers do?" I asked. "Even Zeke would kick Scotty's ass into next month."

One of our older brothers, Zeke, was the lead singer of Wolf Venom, one of the hottest rock bands in the world. He wasn't involved in the family business, but he was as protective of his girlfriend, Abbie, as any of her other six boyfriends were. Including the drummer, Asher DiMarco, Mr D's younger brother.

Yeah, it all seemed a bit incestuous at times.

"Maybe we should give him a second chance," I suggested. "Losing a couple of toes and a lot of dignity, might be enough to teach him a lesson."

Parker peered at Scott's face. "Not to mention the bruising on his pretty boy face."

Scott had a swollen lip and a pair of swollen eyes. His nose was most likely broken.

"I've definitely learned my lesson." Scott looked back and forth between us like he was watching a game of tennis and his life depended on the outcome. This was no centre court at the Australian open. This was far more serious, and a lot more fun.

"Please." Our guest was getting tired. The pleading and the pain was clearly getting to him. His feet must be throbbing like a bitch. The floor underneath was slick with his own blood.

It sucked to be him, as they say. On any given day, I'd much prefer to be me anyway. If I pissed off anyone by touching their woman, and I had many times before meeting Lila, no one would dare to drag Parker or me into one of the sheds beside the Academy building and torture us. Doing that would make them the enemy of our oldest brother, Reuben Brantley. Most people weren't dumb enough to get him offside.

Of course, that meant we got away with pretty much anything we wanted, including fucking other guys' girlfriends.

Of course, after meeting Lila we were one-woman guys, no matter how tempting an offer was.

I glanced at my watch. "We've wasted enough time on this loser. Let's cut him free and get the fuck out of here. I, for one, could use a drink."

I hopped off the table and leaned my hip against it, my arms crossed over my chest.

Parker nodded and gripped the handle of the shears. He yanked them out of the table and stood to snip the zip tie that held Scott's arms behind him. He crouched down and snipped the ones that bound his ankles to the legs of the chair.

"You made a mess down here Scott." Parker clicked his tongue. "You can clean it up."

He grabbed the back of Scott's shirt and yanked him off the chair. He shoved him down onto the concrete floor on his knees and pressed his face down into the puddle of blood.

"Lick it up, asshole," Parker told him.

Scott glanced up at him, but started to lick his own blood off the floor.

For some reason, the sight of the first year student on his hands and knees like a dog, licking at the floor, made me laugh. It was nothing less than he deserved, and it would save washing time later. As a bonus, the floor was rough and not entirely clean. It must be chafing the shit out of his tongue.

That realisation made me laugh harder. It served him right for barrelling around the corridors of Brutham. The moment he laid a hand on Lila, he sealed his own fate. He wouldn't get any sympathy from me or anyone else here at the Academy. We didn't call the place Brutal for nothing.

"This was a good idea of yours, Park," I told my brother.

"I have them once in a while," Parker said. "It's a

shame he didn't piss himself though. I'm sure he'd thoroughly enjoy licking that up."

Scott groaned and gagged.

The sound made my cock harder. I reconsidered the idea of making him suck me off, but dismissed it again. I didn't really need his blood on my balls.

Scott stopped licking and sat back on his haunches. He wiped his mouth with the back of his sleeve.

"It's clean. Can I go now? Please?"

I cocked my head at him. "You know what, Parker? I think I changed my mind about letting him leave."

I slipped a gun out from the side of my jeans, and shot Scott once through the forehead.

CHAPTER 2

HUNTER

"I guess we should call for cleanup." I put my gun away and flicked bits of brain and skull off my shirt.

Parker sighed. Not because he cared whether or not I killed Scott, but because of the hassle that came after. A hassle he put into simple but eloquently resigned words.

"Hunt, we're on cleanup tonight."

"Fuck," I said under my breath. "You could have said something before I shot the prick."

He spread his hands. "I didn't know you were going to kill him. Do I look like a fucking mind reader?"

"You look like me, therefore you should be able to read my mind." I crouched down and grabbed Scott's wrists. "You grab his ankles. Let's get this asshole dealt with."

Parker grimaced. "Why do I have to pick him up by his ankles? You're the one who cut his toes off." In spite of that, he leaned forward and grabbed them before hoisting them into the air.

"You didn't seem to object at the time." We made our way over to the door. I placed the front end of Scott down to unlock and open it.

It was dark out, and quiet. Voices and music came from the Academy building, but down here, near the sheds, there was no one but us.

Unless someone else was down here having fun like we were. That was as likely as not. The sheds were originally built to house animals and gardening stuff, like lawnmowers. When it was turned into Brutham Academy, we appropriated them for different uses. The only animals that came down here now had two legs. However, the lawnmowers were still housed in one of the sheds.

We couldn't have Brutham falling into disarray, could we now?

With Scott swinging between us, we hurried through the darkness and into trees on the edge of the property.

"Hey, *Watch*, turn on the torch," I said roughly in the direction of my wrist.

My watch lit up, illuminating the path through the trees.

"This would be a whole lot easier with a wheelbarrow," Parker remarked.

"Then we'd have to wash out the wheelbarrow," I pointed out. "Besides, this is good exercise. Think how big your biceps would be if we did this every day."

"My biceps are already massive," he bragged.

I snorted a laugh and stopped next to a hole beside some trees. "On three. One. Two."

On three, we swung Scott and hefted him into the hole.

He landed with a thump, half a metre down from the surface of the forest.

"This thing is getting full," Parker remarked.

I shrugged. "When it's full, we'll have another one dug."

"Reuben is going to be pissed off if we keep asking for more money for more holes." Parker walked beside me as we returned to the shed for a pair of shovels.

"Then we'll have to dig them ourselves," I said. "I wish this place would invest in an incinerator. It would be a whole lot fucking easier to drop guys like Scotty inside and not have to worry about him."

"Maybe we can ask Reuben to donate one." Parker grabbed two shovels from beside the door and handed me one.

I accepted it and followed him back out. "And make it easier for us to dispose of the evidence? What would Brutham have to blackmail us with some day?"

They turned a blind eye to anything we did, but there was always something in it for them. Always an angle they could eventually play. If one of us became the head of the Brantley family in the future, we'd owe a very large favour in return for them keeping their mouths shut.

Of course, once we graduated, Reuben would send someone behind us to clean up any evidence. He wouldn't leave that hanging over his head. Ours, yes, not his. If our oldest brother was good at anything, it was covering his ass.

We headed back down into the forest and shovelled dirt from the pile beside the hole, over Scott.

"It would be so much easier to pay someone to do this for us," Parker remarked.

"Easier, but not as satisfying," I replied. "Look at this." I dropped an extra-large shovel full of dirt onto Scott's face, almost completely making him disappear. "Doesn't that feel good after what he did to Lila?"

"Let me try." Parker dropped dirt on the other side of Scott, covering his face completely. "That does feel good. Better than when it's just the kid of one of Reuben's enemies."

Those were all from our first year here at Brutham. Some from before the trials, some from during. Those we dispensed with during the trials, the Academy made us bury ourselves. Something about making us humble, even though we survived the first year here.

"It's true what they say, revenge is sweet." I dumped more dirt on top of Scott and smoothed it down with the back of my shovel.

"It really is," Parker agreed. "It's also making me horny as fuck."

"When are you not horny as fuck?" I leaned the shovel against a tree.

"As often as you," Parker agreed. "Never." He flashed me a grin.

"Exactly," I said. "But there's something about torture and death. It turns me on almost as hard as Lila."

I unzipped my jeans and pushed down the front of my boxers, until my cock sprang free. I wrapped my fingers around my length and stroked my hand up and down until I was hard.

I stood with my feet slightly apart, cock directly over Scott's grave.

In the corner of my eye, I saw Parker pull out his own cock and do the same thing.

I looked away from him and kept on sliding and tugging my hand up and down from my balls to my tip. Pre-cum beaded on my slit and dripped onto the dirt road above Scott's face.

I rolled my hips and pressed my lips together to keep from groaning out loud. The pressure in my balls built to an almost unbearable level. They felt hot, tight and heavy. Begging for release.

Beside me, Parker let out a long, low moan. His movements became faster and faster, before a squirt of cum shot out his tip and over Scott's grave.

Spurred on by my twin, a rush of blood hammered through me and I came, squirting my own cum over the freshly packed dirt. It spread across Parker's, before sinking into the ground.

"That was all kinds of fucked up." Parker tucked his cock away in his pants and did up his zipper.

I laughed softly. "If there's anything we're good at, it's things which are all kinds of fucked up. It comes with being a Brantley."

I shook the last drop off the head of my cock and put mine away too. Coming like this only took the edge off. What I really needed was to sink my cock deep into Lila's pussy and pound her so hard I wrecked her for days. Just the way we liked it.

"It's the best thing about being a Brantley." Parker grabbed up his shovel and lifted it up to his shoulder.

I grabbed my own. "I thought the best thing was being my brother."

"I think they go hand in hand." He shrugged, then broke into a grin. "Or dick in hand."

I laughed louder and offered him a high-five with my spare hand. The best thing about having a twin was getting up to all sorts of shit together. Whatever happened, we always had each other's backs. We never judged each other, not really. We gave each other shit, but when push came to shove, we were a team.

Lila was the last woman we both ever wanted to fuck, but she wasn't the first we both shared. More than one woman had woken up sore from us both.

"As long as you keep your hand off my dick," I told him. We were close, but we weren't *that* close. I was sure women pictured us doing things to each other, but that wasn't our jam.

Besides, we had plenty of women, and men, before Lila; we didn't need to touch each other. With her... She was always willing to go along with whatever we wanted. Neither of us went without.

"Dude." Parker grimaced in the light from a

window at the bottom of the Academy building. "I'd have to find yours first."

I snorted loudly before leaning my shovel up against the wall inside the shed. "My cock is so big, you wouldn't get your hand around it."

"I think you're protesting too much." He leaned his shovel up beside mine and cast a look around the room before stepping over to scoop up the zip ties and duct tape.

"Don't make me use this on you." I picked up the shears and waved them at him before hanging them on a hook on the wall.

"You wouldn't do that," he said easily. "You love me too much. Besides, who else would do this shit with you but me?"

"I'm sure I'd find someone." I draped my arm over his shoulder and gave him a bro hug before shoving him out into the night and closing the shed door behind us.

"Who? Zeke?" Parker laughed. He'd staggered a few steps before finding his footing again. Shame, I would have laughed my ass off if he fell on his knees.

I barked a laugh of my own. "Zeke is nothing but a party pooper. Reuben and Caleb wouldn't want to get their suits dirty. Joshua too. Lucas is too busy fucking… What's her name? Amity Fiorelli."

Parker nodded. "I guess that leaves me. Although,

there's a few guys outside the family who might be fun to hang around with."

I looked at him sideways. "Yeah? Like who? Mr D?"

"Maybe," Parker shrugged. "I was thinking more of his brother, Asher. Or Asher's cousin Ric. Or better yet, the so-called Devils of Dusk Bay."

He spoke derisively, as if they in no way deserved such a cool, collective nickname. I had a fair idea of the shit they got up to. They deserved it as much as we deserved ours— the evil twins.

That nickname started when Zeke referred to us that way to piss us off, but it stuck. Ever since then, we did what it took to live up to it. If anyone was to blame for the things we got up to, it was him, for encouraging us. That's what big brothers were for anyway, right?

"Ice Miller, Ares Turner and Mannix Cassani?" I stepped around the wide fire pit we sometimes used for toasting marshmallows. "I wouldn't turn my back on any of them."

"Neither would I, but I'd fuck their girlfriend, Kennedy. I'd bet you anything she knows how to use her mouth." He smacked his lips.

"I wouldn't take that bet," I said. "Because you have no way of proving it's true. Not without cheating on Lila."

If not for her, Kennedy would be fair game, boyfriends or no boyfriends. She was cute and I did have a thing for redheads. And blondes. And brunettes.

"You might as well bet on Zeke's girlfriend, Abbie." She was also a singer and someone we'd both had unconscious in our esteemed company. Apart from kidnapping her and putting a tracking device in her earring, we hadn't touched her. She was another woman I would totally would have fucked if not for my commitment to Lila. It would have pissed my brother off, but would have been worth it.

I had to be careful. If I kept going like this, Lila might turn me into something vaguely resembling a good person.

I snorted to myself at the thought. As if I could ever be good. Not when it was this much fun being bad.

CHAPTER 3

LILA

I eyed my sister across the table. Since arriving at Brutham, everything had been quiet.

That wouldn't last and we both knew it. Our father made it clear, before we left to come here, what he expected of us.

"One of you will take over as head of the family someday." He'd sat back in his leather chair and regarded us both.

"I expect you to work at proving you deserve it over your sister." He sat forward and rested his arms on his solid mahogany desk. At home, in just our presence, he didn't bother with a suit jacket. The sleeves of his white button down shirt were rolled up to just below his elbows. The face of his chunky Rolex watch caught the light which slanted in behind him from a window overlooking the harbour.

Most people might consider Samuel Bell attractive. Even as his daughter, I saw why.

His dark hair was peppered with grey, but his brown eyes were as shrewd as ever. Power radiated from him. Wherever he went, he attracted attention, especially beautiful women. They flocked to him, enticed by the lure of him and his money.

I'd be naïve if I didn't think he fucked them, but he never kept any of them around for long. Never got attached. After Mum died, he was never with anyone for more than a short while, apart from a brief marriage that ended years ago.

I didn't get the impression he missed any of the women, just no one held his attention. No one was silly enough to think it was because he didn't want anyone getting between him and his daughters. He loved us, but he wasn't sentimental.

"When you say work at proving it?" Chloe asked tentatively.

"Whatever it takes," he said evenly. "This isn't an easy business. If your skin isn't thick enough, you'll be eaten alive. If you let your sister walk all over you, you have no chance out there in the world."

"The trials—" Chloe started.

"You have to make it to the trials first." His eyes took in her, then me. "You know what they say about Brutham Academy."

"It's the only university in Australia with a mortality rate that's higher than the dropout rate," I quoted.

"And do you know why that is?" His expression didn't change.

"To teach us to kill anyone who gets in our way." I was sixteen when I killed my first person, down in the basement of this very house.

I can't claim to have enjoyed it, but I'd do anything for my father's approval and to prove I was a worthy successor to him. If I had to kill again, I would.

But if that person was my sister…

"Yes, but it's more than that," Dad said. He waited for me to elaborate. He was never one for giving us easy answers.

"To stay alive," Chloe said. She gave me the side eye, clearly thinking the same thing I was. She had also killed, but would she kill me if I was in her way? "To make the right connections and allies and use them to further ourselves."

Dad nodded. "Exactly. You're not merely there to learn, although you're there to do that too. You'll both be studying business. Not only will you be in competition for head of the family, you'll be competing academically. Brutham takes your education very, very seriously. This isn't the kind of establishment where you can turn up, not do anything and expect to succeed. Money will not buy a degree from Brutham. Hard work and the right contacts will."

In the corner of my eye, I caught the slight grimace on Chloe's face. She didn't want to study business any more than I did, but we'd both work to excel. We had to. Neither of us was going to hand the position of head of the family over without a fight.

Neither would give the other an advantage of any kind. We were competitive by nature, but the situation Dad put us in made us even more so. We were both equally determined to best the other.

Still, I would have preferred to learn the family business directly from my father. Chloe was the older twin by minutes, but I had what it took to run it. I never hesitated at the things that made her hesitate. Never flinched at things that made her flinch. No one would ever doubt my commitment.

Chloe, on the other hand, would have preferred to take up painting, or playing an instrument, or studying history. Something Dad would definitely not consider to be a worthwhile occupation. A hobby, certainly, but nothing to make a lifelong commitment to.

He'd instilled that in us from a very young age. He wanted us to be well-rounded, but realistic. Useful to the family.

"Something to say?" Dad asked her.

"No," she said quickly. She sat up straighter in her chair. "Nothing."

He cocked his head very slightly. "Good. I don't need to remind you there's a place you can go if you need to think for a while."

She paled. "No, I haven't forgotten," she said quickly.

I had to work to contain a shudder. We both knew what he was referring to.

When he bought this house before we were born, he made rooms underneath it. Several of them. All soundproof, cold and, if he wanted them to be, completely devoid of light.

Built to torture his enemies, both of us spent time in those rooms. So we understood what they were like, he'd explained.

What they were like was a living nightmare. Which was exactly the point. If we put a toenail out of line, the best we could hope for was to only be in there for an hour or two.

Chloe and I did everything we could to avoid going in there at all, but one of his favourite pastimes was sending us down there to give food and water to anyone presently housed there. Thank fuck that didn't happen too often, especially lately. The whole place gave me the creeps.

Dad nodded. "Good. I prefer not to have to put you in those rooms. It gives me no pleasure."

Only the idea of him putting me there made me hold back a snort. He was a Bell. Putting people down in the basement gave him at least *some* pleasure. Even if it was my sister and me.

He liked to cover it with a pleasant smile, and well-dressed exterior, but he had a sadistic streak at least as big as my own. Why else would he have those rooms in the first place? He could just as easily have his enemies killed. He did that too, but the basement was his special, peculiar pleasure.

I lifted my chin. "We'll make you proud. By the time the trials come at the end of the year, everyone will know who is worthy of becoming head of the family. To take your place. In the distant future, of course."

He was harsh, but he was still my father and I loved him. He and I were a lot alike. Ruthless, sadistic and more than a little bit fucked up.

Chloe was all of those things too, but by the time I was done, she'd be begging me to step into our father's shoes.

Dad smirked. "Of course. What you're competing for, may well be for your children to take over from me. I intend to be around for a long time yet."

I smiled, but at the same time I was thinking, *I hope not*.

I didn't want him to die, but I wasn't going to have this opportunity pass me by and go straight to my future children.

No, by the time I was done, I wanted him to know he could retire and leave everything to me. I'd expand the empire he started. I wanted to take the family business global. I wanted to control govern-ments all over the world.

Chloe, on the other hand, would probably want to legitimise the business. As far as I was concerned, that was bullshit. We'd lose millions by doing that. Billions. Who cared about obeying the fucking law? Living and operating outside the law was much more profitable and a fuck load more fun.

"We will definitely make you proud," Chloe said. "The legacy we'll pass on to our children will last for generations."

She didn't mean her children and mine, she meant hers and whoever she got to fuck her pregnant.

I slipped that thought into the back of my mind for later.

"It will definitely be one hell of a legacy," I agreed. "Nothing will stand in our way."

"What are you staring at?" Chloe's voice snapped me back to the present.

I blinked. "Just thinking about that lecture this morning," I lied.

The one advantage of studying the same degree as my sister was getting to talk about it with her. Often she helped to put things into perspective for me. I did the same for her, but that couldn't be helped.

Chloe groaned. "It was so boring. Is there anything more dry than marketing and economics?"

"Your pussy?" I teased.

She grimaced at me. "I'm not discussing my pussy with you. I don't want to talk about yours either," she added quickly. "I certainly don't want to know if it's full of Brantley cum."

"Jealous?" I raised a perfectly shaped eyebrow at her.

"Why would I be jealous?" she asked. "It means I have a better chance of taking over from Dad. As soon as he finds out you're fucking them, all bets will be off."

That was a possibility I'd considered. The rivalry between the two families was vicious at times. My father wouldn't approve of me speaking to them, much less taking them to my bed.

However, as far as I was concerned, the bad blood was between my father and Reuben Brantley. That shit didn't have to continue with our generation.

Hunter and Parker had skills I could make use of, including two skilled tongues and equally skilled cocks. If having a relationship with them put me on the back foot with Dad...I'd just have to work that much harder to get ahead of my sister.

I shrugged one shoulder and pushed my hair back off my face. "Dad will understand. Better than he'll understand you fucking Dane DiMarco. The DiMarco family has no power anymore." Some of them liked to think they did, but in the end they all answered to my father or Reuben Brantley. "How old is he anyway? Forty?"

She glared at me. "He's thirty-four. He's not that much older than me."

I leaned over the table towards her. "Why don't you step aside now? You and Mr D could get married and have a bunch of cute little babies, and leave me to do the real work. Imagine, you could be the wife of a history teacher." If that was all the ambition she had, she had no business competing with me.

"You know as well as I do Dane doesn't want to spend the rest of his life teaching history," she snapped. "He's going to stand by my side when I'm head of the Bell family."

She gave me a venomous smile. "What will you be doing? Spreading your legs for Reuben Brantley's minion brothers? Neither of them will ever have any real power. But you already know that. Honestly, I can't help thinking you're trying to sabotage yourself. Which is fine with me. Maybe *you* should step aside right now."

"I will never step aside willingly," I said coldly. "And I won't let you beat me. It will be Hunter and Parker at my side." I hesitated for a moment. "Or maybe Mr D will change allegiance to me when he realises you're going to lose."

I smiled to myself at the look of doubt in her eyes. I had no interest in Dane DiMarco, but whatever it took to get to her, I'd do it.

CHAPTER 4

LILA

The knock on my bedroom door came early. It always did when it was the twins. All the better for catching people off-guard, according to Hunter.

"Are you decent?" Parker called out through the door.

I struggled to tell them apart at times, but I always knew which twin was which from their voice. Chloe claimed that was bullshit, but I'd never been wrong yet.

"Yeah," I called out. "Come in."

"Shame," Parker said as he stepped into the room, followed by Hunter. "We were hoping to find you naked, lying on your bed waiting for us."

He stepped up behind me and looked at our reflections in the mirror. He cupped my cheeks with his hands before sliding them up my face and tangling his fingers in my hair.

It was almost unfair how good-looking both of them were. One of them that hot would have been unfair, but two? I'd only seen photos of the rest of the family, but all of their brothers were good-looking. Even Reuben, if I was honest with myself.

He and I would make an interesting alliance, if I went there, which I wouldn't. Two Brantley brothers was enough for me.

"What part about that wouldn't be decent?" I teased.

"Good point." Parker gripped my hair and pulled my head back so I was looking up at him. He kissed me with his face upside down from mine. His nose tickled my chin. The stubble from his chin teased the tip of my nose. "Maybe we should stay in tonight instead?"

"I'm not saying that's not a good idea," Hunter drawled. He lay back on my bed and crossed his legs. "But we all know what tonight is. We don't want to miss it, do we?"

He leaned his head against my headboard and looked at us questioningly like he had all the time in the world. If people had past lives, he was definitely a cat. Lazing around in the sun all day, ripping unsuspecting smaller animals apart at night.

"I don't, but..." Parker let go of my hair and slid his hands down the front of my black, V-neck T-shirt. He worked his fingers under my bra and over my nipples.

I shivered. The sensation his touch sent through me was sinfully good. No one would ever accuse me of having a dry pussy, especially around these two. They could make me dripping wet with just a look, never mind their touch.

"We have time for both, don't we?" I asked. "Especially since you're early."

"I'm not saying that's *why* we're early." Hunter grinned. "It might just be a bonus."

"It's totally a bonus." Parker palmed my nipples until I was all but panting. "I bet you're wet as fuck already."

"I bet you're hard as fuck already," I told him.

"Miss Bell, I'm always hard as fuck," he replied. "Especially around you." He drew me up out of the chair and stepped around to press his body against mine. His hard cock poked against my ass. "I will never *not* want to fuck you."

He pulled his hands out of the front of my T-shirt and gripped the hem to pull it over my head.

I raised my arms to help him, but took my T-shirt from his fingers so I could place it carefully over the back of the chair. I intended to wear it later. I didn't need it dumped on the floor and creased.

He unhooked my black lace bra, letting my full breasts fall free. The straps slid down my arms. I caught it before it fell and draped it over my top.

Parker turned me around, admiring my bare breasts while pushing me back towards the bed. He laid me back and let Hunter pull me up until I was lying on top of him.

"You're so beautiful." Hunter lightly gripped my breast in one hand and ran his other through my hair.

"Isn't she?" Parker stood at the end of the bed and looked down at us both. He knelt down beside my ankles and crawled up the bed. He pushed up my skirt, revealing my lacy, black G-string. The front was so sheer he was looking right down at my pussy.

"Gorgeous." He parted my thighs and dove his face straight down between them. He tugged the gusset of my panties aside and went to work on my pussy with his tongue.

"You taste better than honey," he groaned.

"Your tongue feels amazing." I let Hunter manoeuvre me so his upper body was facing me, without dislodging his brother. He kissed my mouth, his tongue sliding over my lips and teeth, before pressing inside.

His tongue was pretty fucking amazing too.

I bent my knees, opening myself wider to Parker before he slipped a finger inside me, then another.

"Definitely wet," he said, his voice muffled by my dripping pussy and clit. "So fucking wet."

I was right on the brink of coming, when he slid his fingers out and lifted his shining face.

"Hey," I protested weakly. I glared down at him, but he only grinned. He knew exactly what he was doing. He could play my body better than anyone else except Hunter. When it came to knowing what I liked, they were equal. Both incredible and addictive.

Parker chuckled and waited until I was almost down from my near-orgasm, before lowering his mouth back to me and slipping his fingers back inside. He worked me inside and out, flicking his tongue against my clit and drawing it between his teeth to bite down gently.

At the same time, Hunter kissed me deeply, thrusting his tongue in and out of my mouth and kneading my breasts with firm fingers.

I loved being with both of them at the same time. Or separately, but there was something about being spoiled like this that I couldn't get enough of.

I closed my eyes and slowly rocked my body in rhythm to Parker's fingers sliding in and out of me, fucking me. Inching me closer and closer to the edge.

Once again, I was almost there and he stopped, pulling out of and away from me. He grinned when I growled, deep in the back of my throat.

"You're such an asshole," I told him.

"Yeah, but you love that about me." He was a cocky prick. But he was right, it was one of the things I loved about him.

I shook my head and glared until he lowered his face back to me. The third time, he only took a matter of moments to get me back to the precipice. If he pulled away this time, I was going to suffocate him with my thighs. Honestly, he might not even mind dying that way. Both guys also had a sadistic streak to match mine. So much so, I knew Hunter would get me off while his twin's body cooled.

Fortunately, Parker didn't pull away this time. He drove me all the way to the edge of the cliff and off the other side, mouth and fingers working me all the way up and not letting up until I came back down.

I sighed against Hunter's mouth and lay against him while I caught my breath.

Parker hooked his fingers into the top of my panties and slid them off. His thumb through one end, fingers gripping the other, he stretched them out and aimed them toward Hunter's face. They hit his twin right in the middle of his forehead. Both of them laughed.

36

I rolled my eyes at them.

"You two are such little boys," I scolded playfully.

"There's nothing little about me, woman," Parker growled, just as playful. He placed his hands and knees on either side of my ankles and crawled up my body. At the same time, he opened his pants. He nudged my knees apart with his and used his hand to position his cock outside my entrance.

Before I could respond to his claim, he sank inside me until he was seated all the way to his balls.

Hunter worked his way out from under me and undid his own pants. "There's nothing small about me either." He nudged the tip of his cock, which already shone with pre-cum against my lips. "Be a good girl and open up for this big boy."

"When have I ever been a good girl?" I asked, but I opened and let him slide his cock into my mouth.

Hunter groaned as he pressed his length almost down to my throat. "Every time my cock is inside you."

"Exactly," Parker groaned. "No one takes my cock as well as you do."

"Or mine," Hunter agreed. "You were definitely made for us." He started to move slowly, sliding in and out between my lips, keeping pace with his twin.

My mouth was too full to respond, so I curled my hand around Hunter's balls and raked over them lightly with my fingernails at the same time as I sucked him hard.

I loved everything about this. The way they both felt inside my body. The way I could control their pleasure with the speed I sucked, licked or rolled my hips. This time, the speed was slow and deliberate. I wanted to drag this out for them the way Parker had with me. I wanted them to suffer the agony of being right on the edge, suspended there until I was ready to let them find bliss.

Nothing in my life made me feel as powerful as this. It was addictive. There would never come a time when I didn't want both of these guys, at the same time or separately.

Parker hooked his hands under my knees and draped my legs over his shoulder so he could pound inside me deeper.

I grabbed a fistful of blanket and dug my nails in. I was on the verge of coming again, but I didn't want to increase the speed, not yet. I focused on breathing and sucking and bucking, until I couldn't take it anymore. I moved faster, pushing all of us nearer.

I was so fucking close. I knew they were too. If I timed this perfectly…

I couldn't stop myself from coming again, but I was only a heartbeat or two ahead of Parker and Hunter. I don't know which of them came first, but it was close enough to almost be in unison. The world disappeared, washed away by panting and groaning, and the rush of blood through my ears.

I arched my back and remembered to breathe while Hunter squirted hot, salty cum down my throat.

"Be a good girl and swallow," Hunter said before easing his cock out from between my lips.

I looked him in the eyes and swallowed every drop.

"So good," Parker groaned. He eased out of me and lowered my legs, but kept my knees apart with his hands. "I'll be right back."

He rolled off the bed and into the small bathroom I had to myself. Fortunately, no one at Brutham had to share unless they wanted to. Otherwise people would get stabbed over things like snoring and leaving clothes on the floor. There was a reason none of the rooms anywhere in the Academy had carpet on the floors. We liked to say it was because cum was hard to get out of the carpet, but so was blood. Not to mention shards of skull and chunks of brain. Hardwood and tiles were much more manageable.

Parker came back a minute or two later with a warm, damp cloth in his hand. He used it to carefully wipe his cum from my pussy.

"Don't want our girl to feel messy, do we?" he asked.

"Not tonight," Hunter agreed. "She'll be messy enough by the end of it."

"Promises promises," I teased.

"We definitely promise." Hunter grinned. "We intend to make you as messy as possible."

CHAPTER 5

LILA

"I love this place," Hunter said. "I think I might keep studying so I can stay here longer."

Academics wasn't the only thing Brutham took seriously. Under the guise of churning out well-rounded adults, they also took the relaxation side to a whole new level. That, or the school board had a lot of kinks they wanted to explore. Either way, that left us with a space to explore. And drink.

The Academy's bar was located in the basement, in a soundproof space that consisted of several private rooms, and one main area with a long bar down one side.

Music thumped from speakers in the ceiling, playing some song that hadn't been released to the public yet. The bass was as heavy as the tone, while the lyrics said something about fucking someone's mouth.

"That doesn't sound like Wolf Venom," I said teasingly. Hunter and Parker had both threatened people with violence in the past if they played their brother's music down here.

I suspected Mr D would be just as happy to hear it as they would. I didn't mind Wolf Venom's music, but it was weird that Hunter and Parker, and Mr D both had brothers in the same band.

In fact, Zeke and Asher were involved with each other as well as with Abbie. Fuck only knew what would happen if Chloe and I started a war between us. Honestly, if it created trouble between Zeke and Asher, that was not my problem.

My interest was in my own ass, as well as Hunter and Parker's. If collateral damage happened along the way, then too fucking bad.

"It's better than Wolf Venom." Parker grabbed my hand and pulled me over to the lounge area in the corner. "It's Blazing Violet. They were the support act for Zeke's band on the last world tour, but now they're headlining. They fucking rock."

"That is the idea of a rock band, isn't it?" I let Parker pull me down onto the couch and settled in on his lap. Hunter disappeared off in the direction of the bar.

"That depends who you ask," Parker said. "For example, if you ask my brother Caleb, he'll tell you rock bands are a really good way of smuggling contraband. Same with hockey teams."

"Hockey teams?" I said with a laugh. "That's specific."

Parker wrapped his arms around me and slipped his hands under the front of my shirt. He pressed them against my belly, and squeezed the soft flesh there.

"Yeah, he bought one." He shrugged. "The Dusk Bay Demons. As far as I can tell, they suck. That's what you get for signing a bunch of guys who come from our... Lifestyle."

"And then they give them knife shoes and sticks, what could go wrong?" I said dryly.

"A puck ton," he laughed.

I jabbed my elbow into his ribs. "That was terrible."

"Hey," he said in protest. He squeezed me tighter. "That joke was awesome."

"You said *awful* wrong," I told him over my shoulder. "Pucking awful."

He groaned. "Now *that* one was bad."

"What was bad?" Hunter approached with a tray in his hands.

43

Another man followed behind him, his gaze on me as he drew closer.

He had to at least have been in his late twenties, with dark hair and blue-green eyes which seemed to see everything. When he looked at me, I got the impression he saw into my soul.

"This is Slade Lincoln." Hunter jerked her head in his direction before placing the tray down on the table. "He's the new business law lecturer."

"Someone had to replace Dexter Clifford," Parker said. He leaned past me to offer Slade his hand. "It's good to see you again, dude."

Slade shook his hand, then sat beside him. "You too, bro."

"You don't sound like a business law lecturer," I remarked.

Slade looked at me appraisingly, his eyes dipping to my breasts and back up again. "I don't? I'm sorry to disappoint you."

"You don't disappoint me," I said quickly. "Just, the last one was uptight and old." This one was young and hot. Looking at him made me want to pant.

"Yeah, I try not to be uptight." Slade already had me naked with his eyes. His fingers were mentally circling my clit.

I swallowed. I had my hands full with the twins,

but there was something about this guy, something compelling. Something as dangerous as them.

"Slade is an old family friend," Hunter said meaningfully.

I guessed as much. He was no innocent who had the misfortune of landing a job here, only to find out what the university was really like. No, he had the air of someone who knew exactly what he was doing.

"I figured he could join us for the evening's proceedings," Hunter added.

"The more the merrier," I said lightly. I managed to drag my eyes away from Slade as several others, also carrying trays, sat down on the couches with us.

Chloe was among them, with Dane in tow. He and Slade exchanged glances and nods before they sat down on the opposite side of the lounge area.

About twelve of us sat around the table, most appearing eager, some nervous.

Satisfied everyone was here, Hunter rose and gestured for everyone's attention.

"Thank you all for gathering here this evening," he started formally. "It's once again time for our monthly game of—" He paused for effect. "Kink or Drink. For those of you who are new to the game—" He nodded toward Slade.

"Allow me to explain how this works. On the trays in front of you, you'll see a variety of delicious shots of alcohol. In the middle of the table, is a stack of cards. The rules are simple. Take a card, read it out loud. You have a choice: do whatever the card tells you, or take a drink. There will be no judgement, whatever you decide. There may, however, be some jeering. All acts must take place in this room, in front of all of us. They may incur some wolf whistles, and possibly some advice."

"I must remind you, cameras and phones are not allowed. Anyone breaking that rule will be taken out and shot." He said the words lightly, but could have meant them literally. As far as I knew, no one ever broke that rule. The game was too much fun for anyone to want to ruin it like that, much less die for it.

"One last thing." Hunter held up his finger. "Everything that takes place here must be one hundred percent consensual. If you cannot find a willing partner for the act the card tells you to do, then you must forfeit and take a drink. If you are so drunk you are unable to perform, you may be laughed at. You will also have to either drink or forfeit. Which is another way of saying 'go to bed.'"

He started to sit down, but stood up again. "I should also remind you, anyone who passes out on the couch is fair game for someone to draw a moustache and glasses on their face." He grinned.

"If you do that to me again, I'm going to whip your ass," Parker growled.

Hunter's grin broadened. "Then don't pass out again, bro. Simple."

Parker flipped him off. "Asshole."

"Guilty." Hunter shrugged and pointed over to a woman on the opposite side of the couches. "Posey, it's your turn to go first."

She gave him a nervous look, but leaned forward and picked up a card. Her eyes widened.

"Get spanked."

"My favourite card." Parker rubbed his hands together.

"I'm fond of it myself," Hunter agreed. "The question is, what is Posey going to do? Kink or Drink?" He gestured at her and gave her a questioning look.

She looked around the table. "If someone wants to…"

"I will." Edward Takahashi seemed quiet and shy when you first met him, but he had ties to the Yakuza, and never missed a game of Kink or Drink. He was always a very active participant. It didn't surprise me he volunteered to spank Posey.

"Ding ding," Hunter said enthusiastically. "Off you go then." He waved them over to the side of the room where a variety of paddles, floggers and various other toys were hung or sat on shelves. "Don't forget the safe word. Banana."

That was the universal safe word for anything that took place here.

Edward waved for Posey to choose her toy of preference. Her gaze skimmed the shelves before she decided on a pink paddle with velvet covering the head and handle. She gave it to Edward before turning around and leaning over the black, vinyl sex couch. That was starting to look well-worn.

She flipped up the back of her short skirt to expose her ass, bare except for a red, lacy G -string.

I glanced over to Slade. He was watching with casual interest, one arm draped over the back of the couch. I couldn't tell what he thought about any of this, but presumed Hunter filled him in before he joined us. This game wasn't for everyone. Better that people knew what they might get into before they took a place on the couch.

Of course, anyone could walk away whenever they wanted to. No one was forced into anything. Pride kept most people from leaving.

I returned my gaze to Posey and Edward as he spanked her ass tentatively with the paddle.

She jumped slightly, but then turned and gave him a smile. In spite of her nerves, Posey wasn't new to the game either. She clearly enjoyed it as much as the rest of us.

"Harder," she said just loud enough to be heard over the music.

He paddled her harder a couple of times on the same ass cheek, before swapping to the other one.

When her cheeks were both red, she turned her face again and said, "Banana."

Collectively we all shouted, "Banana!" We cheered and waited until they sat back down before the next person picked up a card.

That happened to be my sister, Chloe. She leaned forward far enough that her tits looked like they were about to fall out of her dress. She snatched up a card and sat back.

"Fuck the person on your right," she read.

One kink most of us shared in common was that we liked to be watched. That was one of the reasons we were here. Anyone who played this game more than a few times had fucked in front of the group at least once. I had done it several times, as had Chloe.

Unfortunately, Dane was sitting to her left.

She looked at him, then to the guy on her right. He looked keen, but she shook her head.

"Sorry." Dane leaned over to whisper something in her ear, but she shook her head and picked up a shot of tequila. She threw it back and placed the empty glass down on the table.

The guy beside her, Liam, picked up the next card. His face turned pink. "Get blindfolded and fuck whoever volunteers."

"Are you willing?" Hunter asked him, a brow raised.

When Liam nodded his enthusiastic agreement, Hunter gestured at him. "Close your eyes and cover them with your hands. No peeking."

When Liam's hands were safely over his eyes, Hunter waved around the group. "Don't say anything, just raise your hand if you want to play."

Three of the women and two men raised their hands. Posey looked ready to jump out of her seat. Evidently the spanking left her horny as fuck.

"Hands down," Hunter said. "Okay, Liam you're on." He stood and led Liam over to the side of the room. He grabbed a blindfold off the shelf and put it over his eyes. He tied it tightly at the back, then waved at Posey.

Grinning with excitement, she hurried back over to the sex couch and draped herself over it. She flipped her skirt back up again, revealing her bare, still pink ass.

"All right, Liam, over this way." Hunter guided him over until he was standing behind Posey.

Liam lowered his hands as Hunter stepped back, and cupped Posey's ass cheeks. He felt around for a while before he found the top of her G-string. He pulled it down and dropped it onto the floor, then worked two fingers between her legs and over her pussy.

"So wet," he marvelled. He undid the front of his jeans and pushed them down his hips. He positioned his cock carefully before pressing himself into her.

There was something incredibly hot about watching someone fuck someone else, especially knowing he didn't have a clue who it was his cock was embedded inside. Seeing him sliding in and out of her pussy turned me on so hard.

I glanced around the couches to see everyone else watching just as avidly. Every guy had a tent in the front of his jeans. A couple had them undone, their hands inside. They wouldn't work themselves too hard, in case they got a similar card, but they would toy with themselves for a while.

Liam wrapped an arm around Posey and drew her back from the sex couch, far enough to slip his hand between her legs and rub her clit. She arched her back against him, tilted her head and moaned. If he was listening carefully, he might know who she was from that sound alone, but he looked beyond lost to me.

She came first, bucking against his hand, but he quickly followed, pounding into her over and over until he came hard, grunting and groaning.

"Fuck yeah," he said breathlessly. "So fucking good." He held her like that for a while before she slipped away, scooped up her G-string and darted back to the couch. By the time he pushed the blind-fold of his eyes, she was sitting with her legs crossed, looking innocent.

If he asked, we'd tell him who he fucked, but that was up to him. Some people preferred not to know. It was all part of the game.

Liam shrugged and tossed the blindfold back on the shelf before he sat back down.

Hunter smiled at me. "Your turn, babe."

I leaned forward and picked up a card.

I took a breath before reading it. It was a new card. That wasn't surprising. Hunter liked to change them, so we weren't always doing the same things. Some of them were ridiculous, like run around the Academy building naked.

"Fuck someone you've never fucked before," I said. I thought the twins might get angry and pass me a drink immediately. To my surprise, they both gave me speculative looks instead.

"It's up to you, babe," Hunter said. There was a hint of warning in his eyes. If I was going to do this, I better choose very wisely.

I didn't bother to look in Mr D's direction. No one was going to consent to that, even if I was inclined to try. Especially not in front of Chloe.

Instead, my gaze slid to Slade. I knew beyond a shadow of a doubt, the twins would pass me a drink if I chose anyone else here. But him—

"We don't mind sharing if it's with him," Parker said softly.

I raised my eyebrows at Slade.

"I'm game," he said simply.

The expression on his face made me wetter than hell. Yeah, he wanted me.

He put out his hand. I hesitated for a moment before I took it.

He reached over and pulled me until I was straddling his lap. His erection pressed into the side of my leg. The fabric of his jeans was rough against my ass. I undid his fly and pushed myself up enough so he could work his jeans down his hips. I pulled the top of his boxers down with them, freeing his huge cock.

Oh my God.

I glanced over to Hunter and Parker. They both watched with wide eyes, full of excitement and arousal. Not even a hint of jealousy or annoyance. Of course, they were secure in our relationship. They knew nothing would change things between us. This was all about us adding some excitement to it.

I didn't want to see them with another woman, but they were one hundred percent okay with this. That and white hot heat on their faces turned me on even more than before.

I tugged the gusset of my panties aside and lowered my dripping wet pussy slowly down onto Slade's cock.

Holy fuck, he felt so good. I sank all the way down and stayed still for a while before I started to move, rising and falling up and down his cock.

His eyes half closed. "Holy fuck," he whispered. He pulled down the front of my T-shirt and the cup of my bra and kneaded my breast with his hand.

"They look good together," Parker said to Hunter.

"They do," Hunter mused. "I think we might be sharing more often, Park."

Parker hummed his agreement.

That was a conversation for later, but I wouldn't mind enjoying this cock again another time. Maybe even getting to know the man it was attached to.

Slade squeezed my breast. His other hand slid between us to circle my clit. "Come for me sweet-heart," he ordered. "Come for me and then I'm going to come inside your beautiful pussy. I'm going to come inside you while your boyfriends watch us. You want that, don't you?"

"Yes," I said breathlessly.

"I know I do," Parker said. "I want to see you fill her to the brim."

"Me too," Hunter agreed.

And just like that, I was completely undone. I shattered into a thousand pieces, coming hard all over Slade's cock. Blood pounded through me so hard I saw stars in distant galaxies. My whole body sang. I tipped my head back and cried out to the ceiling.

Slade came a few moments later, thrusting hard up into me. "Fuck yes," he panted. "Take every fucking drop. I want you dripping with my cum." He ground up into me, groaning and gripping my breast and my pussy in hard, bruising fingers.

Finally, we both sagged down, slick with sweat and cum.

Between pants, Slade muttered something which sounded like, "I think I'm going to like it here."

CHAPTER 6
LILA

I rounded on Hunter the moment we stepped back into my room. I slammed my hands into his chest and shoved him back a step.

"What the fuck was that?"

He looked down at me for a moment with surprise that quickly passed. His expression turned to one of feigned innocence.

"What was what?" He grabbed my wrists and pushed me backwards into my room.

"You know what." I tugged my wrists free and stomped away from him. I whirled back around and glared. "You put that card there. You knew I'd get it. You were the one who chose Posey to go first. You set me up. You wanted me to fuck Slade."

"You didn't seem to mind." Parker closed the door behind us, but stayed at a safe distance from me.

"You were in on it?" I demanded. I wanted to grab the backs of their heads and bang them together, but at the same time I was angry with myself. I got caught up in the moment and now I was worried about the repercussions. Not to mention the reasons why Hunter put me in Slade's path.

"Since when do you share?" I turned my gaze back to Hunter. He was the one who ran the game. If anyone was responsible for this, it started with him, even if it finished with me. Or finished with Slade inside me.

"We've been sharing since we met you." Hunter grinned as though somehow all of this was funny. When I didn't smile, his faded. "Okay, let's all calm down." He gestured downward with his hands.

"I don't want to calm down," I snapped. "I want to know what the fuck happened."

Hunter sighed and flopped down into the end of the bed. "Chloe had an advantage. Dane DiMarco. Not just his contacts, but his influence."

"Because he's a teacher here?" I already knew how much of that he had. Dane could fail students if he wanted to, or potentially influence his peers to do the same. If I failed any of my classes, that was near enough to an automatic loss against my sister. Now I thought about it, I'd be surprised if he hadn't tried to do that already. Any chance I had of becoming head of the family someday… I could more or less kiss it goodbye.

"Exactly." Hunter leaned back on his hands. "I wanted to introduce you to Slade. You need him in your corner. That card was designed to put all of his attention on you. Which it did. Now he's had one taste of you, he's going to want more. You and your pussy are addictive."

"For the record, it was Hunter's idea," Parker said. He leaned against the door, his arms crossed.

"Thanks, Park," Hunter said sarcastically. He rolled his eyes at his brother, then turned back to me. "I didn't necessarily *expect* you to fuck Slade, but I'm glad you did. Watching you with him was hot as hell."

"Did he know about any of this?" I asked. The idea they might have invited Slade along for the sole purpose of fucking me, made me even angrier.

"Absolutely not," Hunter said immediately. "Like I said, it was meant to be an introduction. Whatever came of it, came of it. I thought you might take a drink, but then you were into the idea, and Parker and I didn't mind." He grabbed my hand and pulled me down to the bed beside him.

"Having a guy like Slade around will give you an advantage over Chloe. With two teachers involved, you'd be on equal footing. With Parker and I, you're miles ahead. Between the four of us, we'll make it so your father has no choice but to choose you."

"What happened to taking people out for coffee?" I asked. "Or lunch. Hell, a nice picnic would have worked too."

"We could have done that, but that would have taken time," Hunter said. "This way, you have us all where you need us."

"You mean *you* have us where you need us," I corrected. "You seem to think you're the one calling all the shots."

He grinned. "Babe, the only thing I'm calling is that your father will choose you. Everything else is a small cog in that wheel. You could have taken a shot and then I would have figured out something else to make sure you had Slade's attention."

"She had his attention the moment he laid eyes on her," Parker said. "Did you see the way he had her naked with his eyes? He was all in like a fish taking the bait. All we had to do was reel him in, and Lila did that with her perfect pussy. The guy never stood a chance."

"Do either of us have a choice in this?" I asked dryly.

"You always have a choice," Hunter said coolly. "No matter what that choice is, we support it. All we want is what's best for you. Now you're on Slade's radar, you'll be able to get him to do all sorts of things. I have a few things in mind myself. I'm not saying you have to have a relationship with the guy, but if you want to, that's fine with us. As long as you don't dump us for him."

I shook my head slowly. My thoughts were tumbling around in my brain.

"You don't mind if I have a third boyfriend?" I asked. "It won't bother you if I fuck him when you're not around?"

"As long as you're not sneaking around, we don't mind," Parker said. "If everyone knows what's going on, where's the harm?"

"Right," I said vaguely. I barely knew Slade. The attraction was undeniable, but fucking someone and dating them were two different things. We might have an actual conversation and realise we hated each other. What would happen then? He wouldn't help me the way Hunter suggested he could.

"Do me a favour. If you find some other guy you think I should fuck, warn me in advance. I feel…"

I slipped my hand out of Hunter's and wrapped my arms around myself. "I don't know. Like I cheated."

"You did not cheat," Hunter said firmly. "If you did, Slade would be missing his cock right now." The expression on his face suggested Slade would be missing a lot more than that. "You're right, I should have told you what I planned, but I wanted it to be spontaneous. Natural. And it was. He wanted you and you wanted him as much as Park and I wanted you to want each other."

He frowned, trying to get his head around that sentence. "You know what I mean."

"We've been trying to figure out a way to pry Dane away from Chloe," Parker said thoughtfully. "He seems very attached. Her too. So far, we've been gentle with them. We have some plans we might have to put into action if they keep going the way they are."

"Does it involve killing either of them?" I asked.

How did I feel about that? Chloe was my twin sister, as well as my rival. We hadn't been close for years, but I didn't *necessarily* want her dead.

Dane, I didn't much care about one way or the other. Students got away with a lot here at Brutham, but killing teachers was usually frowned upon. Hunter and Parker got away with it once, but the Academy would probably fail them if they did it twice.

Their oldest brother Reuben, would be pissed if they flunked out. Especially if it was because of me.

"Only as a last resort," Parker said. "We'll play as dirty as we have to, but killing is way too easy. You want to win because you're the best, not by default. Right?"

"Right," I agreed. If I won because I was the only Bell twin left standing, then so be it, but I really wanted to earn this. I wanted to look my father in the eyes and hear him tell me I was the best of his daughters. The most worthy. The most ruthless.

I ran a hand over my hair and gripped the ends. "Do I want to know what you have planned?"

Hunter laughed. "Probably not. Don't worry, it will be epic. In the meantime, you should get to know Slade. Reel him in a little tighter. We're going to need him to pull a few things off. If he falls for you, great. If he doesn't, he's probably out of his mind, but if you two are friends, that will help too."

"I'm starting to feel like a whore." I gave Hunter a dark look.

"You're a *queen*." He slipped his arm around me. "A queen needs a harem to see to all of her needs. To vanquish her enemies and give her lots and lots of orgasms. Slade can help us at least with the vanquishing, if not the orgasms. With the added bonus of helping you pass business law, which I know you despise."

"You think of everything," I said with a slight touch of sarcasm. "Did you interview all the teachers before you chose him?"

He laughed. "Naw, we really have known Slade for years. He went to school with our brother, Zeke. Come to think of it, he went to school with Dane's brother too, Asher DiMarco. They used to be friends. If they still are, that could work in our favour." He looked thoughtful.

I sighed. "I suppose it can't hurt to try to get to know him. He's kinda hot. And he knows what to do with his cock." And he didn't mind doing it in front of other people. This could make the next game of Kink Or Drink very interesting.

Parker groaned. "I can't decide if I'm jealous or horny. Probably both. If he's better at fucking than I am, I don't want to know."

I snorted a laugh.

"You should be used to being told that by now," Hunter said, looking both sly and cocky. "I've been telling you I'm better than you for ages."

Parker flipped him off. "Yes you have, but it's still bullshit. I'm the one who makes Lila make those cute little panting sounds just before she comes."

"Yes you do," Hunter agreed. "I'm the one who makes her make cute *big* panting sounds. I'm clearly better at getting her off then you will ever be."

He gave Parker the side eye, then turned his gaze back to me. "Park has a point though. If Slade is better than us—"

"You only have yourselves to blame," I finished for him. "You introduced me to him. Whatever the consequences of that, you both have to suck it up." Maybe I could have some fun with this. What was the point of dating hot twins if you couldn't dangle them off the end of a string once in a while?

"Only if Slade lets us," Parker said. He grinned, but his expression was dreamy at the same time. Evidently I wasn't the only one who found Slade hot.

Now I was picturing both of the twins on their knees in front of Slade, taking turns to suck his cock.

"On that note, I need to have a shower." I slipped away from Hunter and stood. "I'm still sticky with Slade's cum." I smiled to myself at the glance they exchanged. Yes, this was definitely going to be fun.

CHAPTER 7
HUNTER

"Keep your eyes and ears peeled." I glanced back to see Parker nod. The best part about having a twin was having someone who always had my back. Some days I felt bad for Lila, because she couldn't say the same about hers.

She didn't have the monopoly on dysfunctional families, but I usually didn't want any of my brothers dead. Not even Zeke that time he held a gun to my head and threatened to kill me. I was almost, mostly, reasonably sure he wouldn't have actually done it, but I was grateful Reuben made him promise not to kill me or Parker at any time in the future. If there was anyone in the world who would keep a promise, it was Zeke. He considered himself above all of the shit our family was into.

Mr Lead Singer of Wolf Venom thought he was

pretty fucking perfect and better than the rest of us. Sure, being a rock star was glamorous and all that shit, but this was much more fun.

I slid the key into the lock and turned it slowly. Like the well-maintained contraption it was, the lock clicked easily and the door opened without a sound.

I glanced around at Parker and grinned. "Good work." He was the one who got the key, made a copy and returned it, without anyone being the wiser.

"You doubted me?" The cocky prick cocked his head at me and grinned. Anyone would think he was the better looking, smarter twin, the way he was acting.

Fortunately, I knew better.

I stepped into the dark room and turned my phone's torch on. We didn't want to be too obvious by turning on the light, or potentially leaving finger-prints. This was by no means our first rodeo.

"If you were a woman, where would you leave your contraceptives?" Parker asked.

My gaze swept the room. It was identical in layout to Lila's, but the bed was covered in blue-grey blankets and pillows instead of the black and red Lila preferred. No clothes lay on the floor here either. No half-damp towels. It was lived in, but not quite as homely.

"If I was a woman, and went to Brutham Academy, I'd probably keep them on me at all times," I said. "In case some nefarious person snuck in and fucked with them."

"Yes, but you're not a trusting person, Hunt," he told me.

"Are you suggesting you are?" I raised my phone and moved it around slowly, taking in everything.

"Not at all," he said with a laugh. "But I know us and what we're capable of. I wouldn't trust us if I was anyone but Lila."

I glanced back at him. "She was pissed about that Slade thing." For a while there I thought we were well and truly in the doghouse with our girl. I never intended to make her feel like a whore. I meant what I said when I told her she was a queen. She was our queen.

Slade could help us secure the crown for her and help her keep it. If he was willing to, of course. Why wouldn't he be? Lila was hot, beautiful and deserving. The whole world should be at her feet, as far as I was concerned. If that meant sharing her with one more guy, then that's what I'll do. Hell, I'd share her with ten more if it got her what she wanted and needed.

I'm not going to lie, I hoped it didn't come down to that. My balls would be so blue they'd probably fall off.

I stepped into Chloe's bathroom. "She might have one of those implant things." I pulled out a handkerchief out of my pocket and wrapped it around my hand before I opened the top drawer.

I smiled. "Bingo." On the top of the draw was half a packet of contraceptive pills. I picked them up and shoved them in my pocket. I pulled out another packet and popped the same amount of sugar pills that she'd already used up, into the toilet.

One by one, they plopped in and sank to the bottom. I flushed the toilet and placed the packet of fake contraceptives in the drawer where the real ones had been.

"Operation fuckery is complete," I declared. I closed the drawer and stepped away from the sink.

"I have to admit, this was a brilliant idea," Parker said.

"Are you admitting that because it was your idea?" I won't lie, I wish I'd thought of it. When I told Lila killing her sister was a last resort, I was sincere. But if Dane *accidentally* got Chloe pregnant, that would throw a spanner in the works.

If nothing else, it might distract her for long enough for her grades to slip. Best case scenario, she dropped out altogether. Samuel Bell wouldn't be happy with her if that happened. Not at all.

Of course, the worst case scenario would be

Samuel Bell embracing his grandchild, and basing his decision on their existence. Although, with a DiMarco as the father, the chances on that were reduced somewhat.

Not as low as they would be if Lila had a child fathered by Parker or me. A Brantley father would not be looked down upon well. That was exactly why we made sure Lila was very careful with her contraceptives. And why Parker and I both had vasectomies. They could be reversed later if we wanted to, but the chances of an unwelcome accident were greatly reduced.

I knew Dane hadn't done the same thing, because I hacked into his medical records and checked. All of this would have been pointless otherwise. Although, breaking into Chloe's room and messing with her was fun anyway. After turning off her security camera, obviously. Neither Parker nor I were born yesterday.

"I might be," Parker said. "It was definitely one of my more inspired ideas."

I turned and raised an eyebrow at him. "Inspired by what? You're not starting to think you want children, are you?"

He grimaced. "Fuck no. I just like to come up with creative ways to screw with people that aren't us. Like Penn that time."

I grinned. Messing with the keyboardist of Wolf Venom was one of the most fun afternoons I'd ever had. The guy was so fucking uptight, he needed some loosening up. The fact he could have died was another item in the 'not my problem' basket. He hadn't died, so no harm was done in the end.

"How long are we going to—" He stopped mid-sentence and froze. "Fuck," he whispered.

Shit, I heard them too. Voices in the corridor outside. Chloe and someone else. A male voice. It sounded like Dane, but I didn't give a crap if it wasn't.

I had a vested interest in whoever she was fucking, but I didn't give a hoot if she was cheating on Mr D.

I dropped to the ground and rolled under the bed as Parker did the same thing. I grunted as he rammed into my shoulder, but fell silent. Now wasn't the time to punch or poke him back.

The door clicked and opened a moment later.

"It's so good to finally get some time alone," Chloe said.

"Tell me about it." That was definitely Dane DiMarco. "It seems like the school board keeps finding things to occupy my time. And yours. I haven't had a moment's peace since the other night's

Kink or Drink. Between that and keeping an eye on that Slade guy..."

The door shut and locked. "Can you believe that?" Chloe asked. "Lila fucking him in front of everyone, including the evil twins."

I grinned at their favourite nickname for Parker and me. If she thought we were evil, she hadn't seen anything yet. Not that she could talk. Behind their backs, people called her and her sister the wicked sisters. They did their best to live up to it.

"When it comes to those three, I'd believe anything," Dane said. "The last thing you need is a guy like Slade Lincoln getting involved with your sister as well. He would complicate things."

Hell yes he would, I thought. *Ain't that awesome?*

"Can we stop talking?" Chloe asked, her tone low and husky.

I have to confess her voice made my cock hard. I would totally fuck Chloe given the chance, and if it didn't complicate things, which it would.

Parker stifled a groan right next to my ear. "Tell me they're not," he whispered.

The mattress dropped to just above my nose as their weight bore down on it. Judging by the sound of wet kissing and zippers, they absolutely *were* going to. And we were going to have to listen to it until we found a chance to sneak out again.

It felt as though only a couple of minutes passed before Chloe started moaning. "Oh my God, your tongue is amazing."

I stuck out mine and made a face at the slats above my head. I would much rather watch than listen and imagine Dane's tongue on Chloe's clit.

On the other hand, the sounds she was making made me harder than hell. I slipped a hand down silently and undid my jeans. I pushed them and my boxers down and curled my fingers around my cock. The harder Chloe moaned, the more she bounced the bed, the harder my hand slid up and down my hot length.

I bit my lip to keep my body as still as I could, and to stop from making a sound. Nothing would give us away faster than screaming when I came.

From the soft but steady pants beside me, Parker was working his own cock.

"Oh, oh, ohhh. I'm going to come," Chloe groaned. "God, yes, right there. Ohhh." Her body went still, but she cried out, long and loud. She sounded a lot like her twin when she was having an orgasm.

The mattress shifted and Dane let out a moan of his own. I pictured him with his cock deep inside her, pumping and grinding. With any luck, he was getting her pregnant right above our heads.

I could be an uncle of sorts to the kid, since I was

so involved in their potential conception. I grinned to myself.

The mattress shifted again. It sounded like they'd rolled over and Chloe was now on top of the history teacher. I bet she got good marks for spreading her pretty little legs for him.

As for him, if I was a teacher here, I'd probably fuck half the students. Was it frowned upon? Sure. Was it illegal? No. Did anyone really give a fuck what went on behind closed doors? Not at all.

Alliances were made and broken against mattresses all over the Academy. It was one of the unwritten rules of Brutham. Don't ask, definitely don't tell. Do whatever you have to do to get through your time here. What doesn't kill you in a place like this will one hundred percent make you stronger. If you don't lose your mind in the process.

"Ride me," he said. "Be a good little slut and make me come."

"Mmm, yes sir," she replied, a smile in her tone.

Fuck, that was hot. Could I get Lila to call me sir? Maybe that was reserved for people like Slade and Dane. That was a conversation that would have to wait until later.

"You're such a good fucking slut." Dane drew out the words as though saying one per thrust up into her pussy. "I'm glad this pussy is mine. You are mine. I… I own you… Ahhh…"

When he came, so did I, hot cum squirting out of my cock and onto my hand and the bottom of the mattress. Oops.

I wiped the rest of it off above my head while Chloe and Dane bounced around for a while longer. By the time they went still, so did I. I closed my eyes and sighed. We'd have to wait until they left or fell asleep before we could sneak back out again.

It might be a long, uncomfortable night under here.

CHAPTER 8

LILA

"What the hell did you do?" Chloe waved something in my face.

Apparently she didn't give a crap that we were in the middle of a busy corridor outside the library. A couple of students stopped to stare. We both glared at them until they hurried away.

I grabbed her wrist to take a better look.

"What the hell?" I squinted. "Why are you waving contraceptive pills in my face?" I shoved her wrist away from me.

"They're not contraceptive pills," she snarled. "Someone changed them out."

I snorted a laugh. "It wasn't me. Don't tell me you're pregnant."

"Thankfully not." She lowered her hand to her side. "I noticed they'd been moved slightly and got suspicious. I had the Academy lab look at them. They're nothing more than sugar." She looked at them in disgust before flinging the packet into a rubbish bin.

"Maybe Dane did it," I suggested. "That sounds like the kind of thing he'd do."

It also sounded like the kind of thing the twins would do. If they had, they hadn't told me. They were going to have some questions to answer when they got back from yet another business trip for their brother, Reuben. He usually sent them during the holidays, but once in a while something 'urgent' came up that only they could handle.

The last time, Parker came back with a broken nose and some story about an unprovoked attack by an asshole he wouldn't name. Apparently it was better if I didn't know. Sooner or later, I'll get him or Hunter to tell me the details. For the time being, I was content to let it lie.

"Dane wouldn't do that," Chloe said, but she looked uncertain. "Are you sure it wasn't you? Some kind of fucked up way to try to get to me? Did you think I'd get pregnant and drop out of Brutham?"

I raised my hands to either side. "I had nothing to do with it. If I did, I would have put something stronger in them than sugar. Nothing would get you kicked out of the Academy faster than taking illegal drugs."

They didn't care if we got drunk off our faces, or stabbed each other, but they drew the line at drugs.

Chloe growled. "Fucking bitch. That is something you'd do, isn't it? Or something you'd have your lap dogs do. No wonder you and they get along so well. You're all degenerates. You'll bring the Bell name down into the gutter."

I rolled my eyes. "You'd know all about the gutter. It's the favourite place of most people with the last name DiMarco. You know the only reason Dane is with you is for his own ambition, right? He'd suck Dad's cock if it got him power. Or Reuben Brantley. Hell, he'd suck them both and call them ice cream if they threw him half a bone."

Her face turned pink. "Dane has more integrity than you ever will. He—"

"What's going on?"

I didn't know Slade was there until he stood beside me.

He looked from me to Chloe and back again. "You two are getting loud."

Chloe regarded him for a moment and forced a smile. "Sorry, sir," she said with saccharine sweetness. "My dear sister and I got a little carried away. We didn't mean to be a bother." Past all the mock sweetness, she was giving him 'bend me over your desk and fuck me' eyes.

Would she really do that? Potentially.

She might have the kind of relationship with Dane that I had with Hunter and Parker. The kind where they didn't mind sharing, and were ambitious for me. Slade taught my weakest subject. It would be an easy matter for him to fail me if Chloe got him on her side.

The prospect should have made me nervous, but it was pushed off my radar by the idea of them together. That gave me an unexpected stab of jealousy right in my heart. My competitive nature flared, along with my anger.

If Slade was going to be with either of us, it would be me. I'd make certain of that.

"Chloe was just wrongfully accusing me of tampering with her birth-control," I said frankly.

He gave her a long look, then turned his gaze to me. "Did you?"

"I can one hundred percent promise I did *not*," I told him. "I don't know who did."

I had a fair idea, but I wasn't exactly lying. I *didn't* know for certain. He understood that as well as I did.

He rubbed a hand over the stubble on his cheek. "I'm sure you appreciate what the penalty would be for doing something like that."

His gaze seemed to bore right into me, stripping off my clothes and a layer or two of skin. He was definitely not talking about expulsion. The punishment he had in mind probably involved a paddle and restraints.

My tongue darted over my lips. I was wet as hell thinking about it. I almost wished I *had* changed Chloe's pills. Let him spank my ass until I screamed for him to stop. And then a few more times after that.

"Yes, sir." I looked at him through my lashes. "The punishment would be very severe. I would feel the repercussions for days." Including a pussy so wrecked I wouldn't be able to walk for a week.

His eyes darkened. Hell yes, he was thinking exactly the same thing I was. With Hunter and Parker away, I was already suffering from a terrible case of blue clit. If he kept looking at me the way he was, I was going to come right here in the middle of the corridor.

Chloe made a sound of disgust. "Just so you know, I've already had the lock on my door changed. And the code to access my security camera. Whatever it takes to keep myself safe." She gave Slade a last smile before she turned and walked away down the corridor, ass wiggling as she went.

"I love her, but she can be so paranoid." I sighed

dramatically. "Anyone would think I'm out to get her."

"Aren't you?" Slade asked bluntly. Before I could respond he pressed a finger to his lips to signal silence. "Let's not talk about it here. Come with me to my office."

I didn't miss the double meaning. If he wasn't careful, I was going to start dripping down the insides of my thighs.

"Yes, sir." I walked beside him down the corridor and into another one that led to the back of the Academy building. A lot of the teachers had offices here, with views that overlooked the lake and the forest beyond.

He gestured for me to step inside and closed the door behind us.

"I think you have some explaining to do." He leaned against the edge of his desk and crossed his arms. He made no attempt to hide the tent in his pants.

"What do you want to know?" I crossed my arms too and pushed my breasts up higher. His gaze dropped to them before flicking back up to my face.

"That whole Kink or Drink game. Was it set up?"

"Yes it was, but I wasn't in on it," I replied. "Were you?"

His expression faltered for a moment. He clearly

hadn't expected me to throw the question back at him like that.

"No. I've known Hunter and Parker for years. Hunter invited me along for some fun. What happened between us... It was unexpected."

"Yes it was," I agreed. "It was a spur of the moment thing. Do you regret it?"

"No," he said immediately. "The opposite. The moment I saw you, I was drawn to you. Like a moth to a dangerously hot flame." The side of his mouth twitched. "All I could think about was touching you, fucking you. When I realised you were the twins' girlfriend—"

"You figured that was that?" I asked.

He worked his mouth into a slow smile. "No. I figured I'd have to find a way to steal you away from them." He lowered his arms and stepped towards me. "The minute I saw you, I decided you were mine. Whatever I had to do, I would have found a way to make that happen."

His smile became boyishly lopsided. "Students go missing all the time around here. If it came to that..."

I should have been as disturbed as hell to hear him say he would have killed Hunter and Parker to win me, but it was hotter than fuck. What girl doesn't want a guy who's prepared to go to great lengths for her?

"And now?" I asked.

He cupped my face with his hands. "They seem all right with sharing."

"They are." I locked my eyes on his. If I wasn't dripping before, I was now.

I took a steadying breath before things got out of control. "Hunter and Parker had an ulterior motive for introducing us to each other." I quickly explained the rivalry between Chloe and me and the reason for it. And why the twins thought Slade could help.

"If you want to walk away right now, I understand," I told him. The electricity crackling between us was undeniable, but the reality was we were playing a dangerous game. A game that wasn't for everyone.

"You don't understand." His voice was barely above a whisper. "The moment I saw you, I couldn't walk away. Whatever this is between us, I want that and everything that goes with it. If that means doing some dubious things…" He shrugged. "It wouldn't be the first time. I teach law, but I've broken plenty of them. But that's a story for another time. I need you."

He dropped his hands to my hips, turned me around and pushed me until I was bent forward over the top of his desk.

He flipped up my skirt, pulled my G string aside and slid two fingers straight into my soaking pussy.

"You are so fucking wet," he marvelled. "How badly do you want me?" He slid his fingers in and out, stroking my flesh and threatening to drive me wild.

"Badly," I panted. "So badly, sir."

"I like the sound of that." He grabbed a fistful of hair and pulled my head back while he continued to fuck me with his fingers. "Do you want my cock?"

"Yes. Yes I do. Please, sir." The blood was racing so fast inside me I could barely think or breathe. I needed to have his cock inside me so, so much.

"If you want my cock, you have to earn it," he said. "You have to come for me." He slipped his fingers out and turned his hand so he was rubbing the heel over my clit. He slid his fingers back inside and worked me harder than ever.

I placed my palms down to the desktop to either side of me, my chest pressed against the cool wood. I spread my legs as far as they'd go, opening me out to him further.

"I'm going to come, sir," I said between breaths.

"Good, come… Right now."

His demand pushed me over the edge immediately, as though my body had no choice but to obey his order. I groaned into the desktop as he worked me all the way through my orgasm and back down the other side.

I lay puffing lightly and trying to get my breath as he slipped off my G string and replaced his fingers with his massive cock. He eased into me slowly, giving my body time to get used to him.

"All my cock has wanted to do since the other night was get back inside your body." His voice was low and husky with desire. "I'm going to fuck you everywhere. All of your holes are going to be mine. But for now, I'm going to claim your pussy. I may have to share her with two other cocks, but right now, she belongs to me." He pushed himself all the way inside me until he was seated to his balls. He placed his hands on the top of the desk beside me and started to thrust slowly.

He took his time, fucking me with slow, even strokes, savouring the sweet friction between our bodies. Fucking me into the oblivion of a second orgasm before he joined me, tipping over the edge and filling me with his cum.

He slipped his arms around me and pulled me up while his cock was still deep inside me. He buried his face in my hair and inhaled deeply.

"This is just the start," he promised.

CHAPTER 9
LILA

Parker handed me a drink and flopped down beside me. How he managed not to slosh beer over the side of his glass, I have no idea. He had an interesting skill set.

"So Chloe figured it out, hmmm?" Hunter reclined in a chair opposite us. A private room in the Academy bar was a favourite place for us to drink and plan world domination.

"So it would seem," I said. They told me how they snuck into her room, changed her contraceptives and spend half the night under her bed waiting for her and Dane to stop fucking and fall asleep. They'd managed to sneak out again a couple of hours before dawn.

Both of them thought it was hilarious. So did I, but at the same time, it served them right, getting stuck under there. Without doubt, they'd do it again. They were slightly out of their trees, but that was part of their charm. There was nothing they wouldn't do for shits and giggles.

"She was definitely not happy about it." Slade sat in a chair beside Hunter. He looked at us over the rim of his glass. He'd grinned when the guys told their story. If he was bothered by it in any way, he showed no sign. If anything, he seemed to admire the twins' audacity.

"The question is, what do we do next?" Parker asked.

"I recommend practising for the trials," Slade said. "We can deal with whatever Chloe throws at Lila, but during the trials, there's only so much we can do. The more prepared you are, the better. You'll be able to focus on going after her, or protecting yourself, rather than on the trials themselves."

A flutter of fear passed through me. The trials were Brutham's way of separating the stronger students from the weaker. The ones with strong connections from the ones without.

During the trials, we'd be taken to a particular location. From there, we had to make our way to another location. That was it. In terms of rules, there were none.

If anyone got in our way, we could remove them.

By any means. The trials were often used as a way for students to resolve past grudges. Few students who survived the trials came out of it unscathed.

"I should know what to expect, I suppose," I said slowly. I could ask them for help, but if Chloe came after me somewhere remote, they may not get to me in time. And vice versa. Slade was right. The better prepared I was, the more chance I had of getting through the trials in one piece.

"We'll make it fun for you." Parker grinned. "By the time the trials come around, you'll be looking forward to it."

"That sounds like a big ask to me," I told him. Excuse me for being sceptical. Cynicism went hand in hand with being a Bell.

"Do you trust us?" Hunter gave me a searching look, although his tone was light.

"Yes," I said without hesitation. "Of course I do." They hadn't blinked an eye when I told them I fucked Slade in his office. Or when I included him in this meeting. It felt natural to have all three of them here. Like Slade was the final piece of our puzzle.

"Then trust us when we say we can make this good for you," Hunter said. "We've all been through the trials, we know what to expect."

"You two had each other's backs," Slade pointed out. Not accusing, just stating a fact.

"That's true," Hunter conceded. "But Reuben has a lot of enemies who would have paid to have us eliminated."

"It just so happens, we're smarter, faster and more resourceful than they were." Parker looked smug. "They were never going to catch us."

"So I may have more than Chloe to contend with." I grimaced. "My father has some powerful enemies too, including Reuben."

"Any chance Reuben would pay you to eliminate Lila and Chloe?" Slade asked bluntly.

"There's every chance he'd try," Hunter agreed. "There's no chance we'd take it."

"Does he know that?" Slade cocked his head at the twins.

They exchanged glances.

"He does," Parker said carefully. "Zeke was nice enough to fill him in on that. He's not happy, but we're still alive, so I guess he still needs us for…things."

"He wouldn't have made Zeke promise not to kill us if he didn't need us for, like Parker said, 'things,'" Hunter agreed.

"Like potentially killing Lila and Chloe?" Slade pressed a little harder.

"Chloe maybe." Parker shrugged. "But only if we have to, not because our brother paid us to do it. If we have to choose between Lila and him, we'll choose her every time. If she needs Chloe dead, then she'll be dead." He nodded as though that was the end of the conversation.

Hunter sat forward, forearm across his thighs supporting his weight. "I know what you're trying to do. You want to know exactly where our loyalties lie. They're with Lila. Where are yours?"

"You're the one who brought me in here," Slade pointed out.

"Answer the question," Parker said. His eyes narrowed dangerously. He smiled a lot, but sometimes it was good to remind people he was as dangerous as fuck as well.

Slade matched Hunter's pose. "In the same place. My loyalty is with her. I'd like to think the four of us are a team. With one ultimate goal. Lila's happiness."

"And giving her lots of orgasms," Parker added.

Slade sat back and smiled. "Definitely lots of those."

"Are you all done?" I asked. "Would you like a moment to pull out your cocks and compare them for size?" This conversation was gratifying and in some ways necessary, but it wasn't getting us any closer to making any plans. Not that I didn't appreciate every single one of those orgasms.

"No need, we all know Slade's is the biggest,"

Parker said. He didn't seem too concerned about the fact. "Mine isn't as big, but I know how to use it." He glanced over at me and grinned.

"Yes, you do," I told him. All three of them did. Better than any other guy I ever fucked.

With the possible exception of my stepbrother Zachary. The only guy, as far as I knew who both Chloe and I screwed. Thinking of him reminded me of my stepmother. She and my father weren't together for very long, but we got along well enough. When she left my father's life, she left mine as well. Only Zachary stayed in contact these days.

"Apart from the trials, what else can we be focusing on?" Hunter asked.

"I've offered to tutor Lila," Slade said, looking smug. "And by that I mean actual study as well as orgasms. I'll make sure no one has any excuse to fail her."

Hunter nodded. "That's a good idea. I'd suggest you try to make friends with Dane, but I doubt he'd take the bait. If he doesn't know you're also involved with Lila, he soon will. Shame, we could have used someone keeping an eye on him. He's a slippery fucker."

"I'm sure he could say the same about you," Parker said.

"That's because I am a slippery fucker," Hunter

agreed. He grinned. "I know the kinds of things we get up to, which makes me nervous. After what we did to Chloe's birth control, we can expect them to do something. They're not going to take that lying down."

"Any idea what they might try?" Slade asked. He sipped his beer, with his brow creased in a slight frown. He was sexy as fuck when he was that intense.

"Chloe likes to sell herself as the nicer twin," Parker said. "If she does something, it's going to be something subtle. Preferably something she can pin on someone else."

"That's exactly what she'd do." I sighed softly.

I hated having to be wary of my sister. I would have loved a relationship with my twin like Hunter and Parker had.

Although, if they were pitted against each other, it would get even uglier than this. They had no filter, or much in the way of a moral compass. What was the expression? Morally grey. My guys were closer to morally charcoal; so dark they were almost unforgivably bad.

To people who weren't me and now Slade anyway. I loved them all the more for it.

I'd hate to have them off side. Chloe must lie awake at night wondering what they'd do next.

Honestly, I doubted there was anything *close* to a limit to what they might pull.

Parker wrapped his fingers around mine. "Whatever happens, we'll deal with it. She's not getting past us to get to you. And if she does, we'll deal with that too. The four of us are an unstoppable force. Sometimes for good, sometimes for evil." He grinned.

Hunter frowned at him. "When are we a force for good?"

"Whenever we have our tongues on Lila's clit," Parker retorted. "Or our hands. Or our cocks. Or a vibrator, for that matter. Any time we're giving our queen orgasms."

Hunter pointed a finger gun at him. "You have a point, bro. That's definitely good."

"Of course I have a point," Parker said. "I am the smarter twin." He pretended to fluff the back of his hair.

"In your dreams," Hunter said with a laugh.

I turned to Slade. "Do you have any siblings?" He'd been watching the conversation with a combination of curiosity and amusement. Like a guy would watch his younger siblings banter and squabble. I realised I knew almost nothing about him.

"I have two sisters," he replied. "One older and one younger. Kirsten and Darcie. They don't get along very well either."

"You went here, to Brutham?" I sat against the back of the couch and crossed my knees.

"I did, yes," he agreed. "We all did. I… I had an older brother who didn't survive the trials. He got too cocky and made too many enemies. That put a lot of pressure on us to succeed. Everyone assumed we'd be like him. But we all got through and we're stronger for it."

"What do your sisters do?" Parker asked. He pulled my feet onto his lap and took off my shoes. With his drink in one hand, he started to massage my toes with the other.

"Kirsten works with Mack D'Antonio, the businessman," Slade said slowly. "Darcie works for the twins' brother, Caleb. They're both ambitious and career driven."

I nodded. I'd never met either man, but I knew *of* them. If Slade's sisters worked with or for them, then they were as up to their eyeballs in this lifestyle as I was. None of which I could or would judge them for.

Although, neither were fans of my father, so we may end up rivals someday. Or, if I had my way, we'd merge everything Bell with everything Brantley. If we could achieve that, we'd be virtually unstoppable. Above every law and government. Rich beyond most people's wildest dreams.

"How receptive are they going to be when they

learn about your current situation?" Hunter turned his pointer finger around in the air in a circle, to gesture to all of us.

Slade shrugged indifferently. "They'll deal with it or they won't. That's a bridge I'll worry about when we get to it. But on a woman to woman level, they'll adore Lila. They love women who are as tough, independent and smart as they are. If nothing else, they will respect you." He nodded to me.

"They better," Parker growled. "Lila deserves all the respect she can get."

"And then some," Hunter agreed.

I sipped my drink and smiled at them. They were right. Whatever Chloe threw at me, we'd be ready for it. How could I not be with three incredible, hot guys on my side.

CHAPTER 10
LILA

"Where the hell are we?"

We were at least an hour from Brutham Academy, deep in the bush. We could bring people out here, bury them and they'd never be found. On the other hand, neither would we if we got stuck out here.

"This is where the trials are held," Slade said. "Technically only people who have been through them before, or who work at the Academy should know the whereabouts of this place. Of course, some rules are meant to be broken more than others."

"And frequently are," Parker said. "We're not the first to bring people out here for this."

"We won't be the last," Hunter agreed. "But we are going to have the most fun."

"Getting me lost in the forest?" I eyed the trees

doubtfully. The Academy was situated in a nice setting, with countryside all around it, but I was a city girl at heart. This kind of bushland was not the kind of place I frequented. I preferred my wildlife in the form of the three guys who stood around Slade's SUV, each looking hot and cocky.

"We are not getting you lost," Slade assured me. "You have a compass on your watch. All you need to do is head east. The location you need to reach is only five kilometres that way." He jerked his head.

"Only," I echoed. It would be slow going with heavy scrub, rocks and fuck knows what else. "It's all fun and games until I run into a yowie."

"If they exist, you won't find them here," Hunter said. "Past trials would have scared them off. You might see a fox or two, but they'll run from you." He folded his arms around me and pulled me to him. "The only predators around here are us."

"That's where the fun part comes into it," Parker said. He rubbed his hands together. "We'll give you a head start before we give chase."

A flutter of excitement passed through me. I should have known they planned something.

"What happens if you catch me before I get to the finish line?" I asked.

Parker grinned. "Whoever catches you first gets to fuck you."

"And if two of you catch me at the same time?" I asked.

"Then we both get to fuck you," Hunter said. "And the unfortunate guy that gets left behind has to watch." He sounded very certain that wouldn't be him.

Were they giving me incentive to run, or stick around and have a good time? My competitive instincts quickly kicked in, overriding any doubt or hesitation. That rush of adrenaline that lit me on fire. I wanted to beat them all. I wanted to stand at the finish and laugh at their expressions as they saw they were beaten by a woman.

"And what if I get to the finish line before any of you catch me?" I raised my chin in challenge.

"Then you win our undying admiration and we all get to fuck you," Hunter said. "It's a win-win situation for everyone."

"You're not going to be competing with each other, are you?" I asked. The last thing I needed was for them to injure or maim each other so they could keep up with me.

"If you're asking if we have dirty tricks to pull on each other, the answer is no," Hunter said. "At least, nothing specific. If I happen to trip either of them over, then so be it."

"The point of this is so you have a feel for the

landscape," Slade said. "The rest is a bonus, to take the pressure off you. If we do this enough times, you'll reach the finish line within an hour or so, hopefully bypassing any trouble. The rest of the students will be busy getting lost and causing problems for each other. By the time they realise you're not, you'll be long gone."

"Not just that, but you may see places you can use to your advantage," Hunter said. "Places where you can deal with Chloe if she tries anything."

"Dane is going to bring her out here for the same reason, isn't he?" I asked.

"Highly likely," Slade agreed. "All the more reason to know where she may set traps for you."

I made a face. "Other universities just have exams." Which were their own special kind of hell. Brutham had them too, but this on top of those? It was next level torturous pressure.

"Other universities don't turn out students who are ready to deal with everything life throws at them," Hunter said. "Brutham is brutal, but those who survive are tougher and smarter than anyone else. It's easy enough to pass an exam. It's a lot harder to survive each other. Do that, and you'll be unstoppable."

"I know." I sighed. "It's just... Extreme. Who came

up with this anyway? Whoever they are, they're a sadistic fuck."

All three of the guys grinned.

"They really were," Slade agreed. "But there's no feeling like crossing that finishing line and knowing you survived your first year. You feel invincible."

"Slade is right," Hunter said. "It feels amazing. But today will feel even more amazing. And don't worry about getting lost. We put a tracking device in your watch and a backup one in your earring, just in case."

He frowned briefly. "It might be worth putting one in a clit piercing as well. In case someone tries to pull them out during the trial itself. A few people last year had piercings torn straight out. Most won't think to look at your clit."

"They better not," Parker growled. "I'll push them off a fucking cliff if they go anywhere near her clit."

"Get in line, bro," Hunter told him.

"We can push them together," Slade said placatingly. "Hunter is right though, a clit piercing would be a good idea. Not *just* to have somewhere to put a tracker though." He grinned.

"Only if you get a cock piercing," I said to all three in general. I'd get a clit piercing if it meant not getting lost out here, but I'd never thought about getting one for any other reason.

"I will," Parker said immediately. Of course he did, he was the more adventurous of the twins. It must be a younger twin thing. I was the same way, where Chloe was the predictable, reliable twin. At least, that was the picture she painted of herself to the world. I'd seen her do some pretty wild shit in the past. Nothing I wouldn't do though. I preferred to take life by the balls and live it.

"In the meantime, let's get this hunt started before the sun goes down." Hunter jogged on the spot to warm up. He gave me a predatory look that set my blood on fire.

I forgot I was going to be running through trees and bushes and started to see it for what it was. Something primal. Three gorgeous guys chasing me, hoping to catch me and pin me down under their bodies. I was the rabbit and they were the hungry wolves, desperate to sink their teeth into my flesh. To tear me to pieces. To wreck me completely.

I nodded. "How much of a head start do I get?"

"Five minutes." Slade glanced down at his watch. "Your time has started, little bunny. If I was you, I'd run."

If he thought he was going to give me the nick-name 'little bunny,' we'd be having words later. In the meantime, I pressed on the compass on my watch, turned until I was facing east and started to run.

I didn't look back until I reached the line of trees. All three of the guys stood side by side, backs to the SUV, arms crossed. Each was trying to give the impression he was relaxed, but the tension in their bodies said otherwise. They were ready for this, as though they chased women through forests on a regular basis. As though they were just doing this for fun, but for the continuation of the species. Only the strongest, fastest, smartest got to fuck.

I smiled. Only if they could catch me.

I turned away and ducked down into the trees.

It was a good thing I was dressed for this, in solid boots, jeans and a sturdy long sleeved shirt. Anything else would have been ripped to shreds on the branches as I ran past. I would have tripped in the kind of shoes I usually preferred. If they really wanted to torture us, they'd make us do the trials in heels. That sounded like the perfectly sadistic thing whoever came up with this would do. Assholes.

I held my hands up in front of me, protecting my face and sweeping branches away in front of me. Every so often, I glanced down at my watch to make sure I was still heading in the right direction. I had to turn to the south to run around a particularly thick section of bush.

The moment I could, I headed back east, I turned but slowed to a quick walk. Running through the trees sounding like a herd of elephants would be the quickest way for the guys to find me.

I glanced back a few times, but saw no sign of any of them. Once in a while, I heard a shout that suggested they were following quite a way back.

Good, I thought. *Stay back there*. I was not going to let them catch me. I had to be fast like that little bunny, but I also had to be smart. Outrunning them wouldn't be enough. I had to think like them. What would they do?

Parker would barrel on through the trees, shoving anything and everything out of his path. He'd want to head in a straight line and hope to catch me in the middle of it.

Hunter would live up to his name. He'd be looking for signs of the direction I went, tracking my every move and trying to anticipate where I'd end up next. He knew the terrain. If he saw me skirt around the thick bushes, he'd know where the next one was and figure out the best way around them.

I might outrun Parker, but I'd have to out think Hunter.

Slade— He was the most difficult one to figure out. He zeroed in on me the moment we met. He knew what he wanted and set his sights on getting me. He'd also done the trials before, and knew the terrain.

I mulled it over for a minute or two before I realised. I knew where he'd be. I'd have to be very careful to avoid him.

I reached a place where several large boulders stood in my way. On the other side was a drop down into the valley below. It was exactly the sort of place I wouldn't want to be pinned down during the trials. A couple of people wanting to dispose of me and I'd be pushed down off that drop. If the fall down the sheer rock didn't kill me, the landing would.

The question was, how did I get past?

Almost as soon as I had that thought, I had another realisation. It wasn't just how I got past, it was about how the guys *expected* me to get past. They'd be waiting for me to reach places like this. They'd be expecting me to behave in a certain way. I had to do something unexpected. For the first time, I understood the point of the trials. It wasn't just a test of loyalties and who wanted who dead, although it was also that, it was about using critical thinking skills.

I stepped back and crouched down in some bushes.

Directly east was straight over the edge of the cliff. In order to get by, I had to work my way around the ridges on either side. One looked easier to navigate than the other. The easier way would be the logical choice.

I turned towards the more difficult ridge.

CHAPTER 11

HUNTER

I took my time following Lila through the thick forest of gum trees. I loved the smell of them, and the way the scent clung to clothing and hair. We'd all smelled like dirt and sweat and gum trees after this. Earthy and real.

Don't get me wrong, I liked civilisation and city living as much as the next guy, but there was something compelling about being here in nature. Hunting down our mate like a pack of wild animals.

Parker was moving through the trees a few metres to my south, sounding just like that. A pack determined to trample everything in his path. I adored my twin, but he was about as subtle as a hippopotamus on steroids.

Slade was somewhere to the north. At least, I presumed he was. He drew the short straw and had to leave last. He'd looked so smug, I was sure he had a plan to get around us somehow. Or maybe that was what he wanted us to think. That was all part of the game. It wasn't just a chase, it was also a mind fuck. My second favourite kind of fuck. Unless it was my mind getting fucked with.

Either way, I wasn't going to let him psych me out.

I reached a thick section of bushes and tracked Lila's movement around them. Here and there were snapped twigs and sections of disturbed ground coverage. At this time of year, the leaves were thick on the ground and dry. The signs they left behind were almost as good as a neon arrow pointing the way.

I smiled to myself. Lila couldn't be too much further ahead. When I caught up to her, I was going to pin her cute little ass to the trunk of a tree and fuck her silly. I was going to fuck her so hard, the other guys would hear her scream from kilometres away.

They could listen all they wanted. She was going to be my prize. The hunter would catch and claim his prey out here in nature.

This whole thing was so primal, it set my blood on fire. I was so hot it didn't bother me that until now I hadn't thought to insist Lila wear a remote control vibrator as she ran. I made a mental note to include that next time.

If she had one inside her now, I'd turn it on and grin at the sound of her squealing. That would slow her down like nothing else.

I pushed on through the trees until I reached the boulders. I stopped for a moment to reminisce about the trials. Parker and I had cornered Brinson Smith here. The smug prick was on our radar for quite some time. He seemed to have a thing for every woman we set our sights on. Back then, it was nothing serious, just a fuck here and there, but he was always hanging around.

Not after the trials he wasn't. I gather it was a difficult process to recover his body from the bottom of the cliff.

"Sorry not sorry," I said to myself. Seeing the expression on his face as he scrambled to grab on to something, anything, only to be shoved backwards by Parker, was one of my most satisfying memories. If we hadn't done it then, we would have had to do it later. He would definitely have been sniffing around Lila. No one did that and got away with it, unless we'd agreed upon it. Which, apart from Slade, we never would. One of our many mottos was 'touch her and die.'

Fortunately, Slade agreed with that sentiment.

Lucky for all of us, we didn't view each other as rivals, or shit would get really ugly really quickly.

"Now, which way would you go?" I asked Lila under my breath. One of the ridges was easier to navigate than the other. I would bet anything she realised the same thing. And that I would expect her to take the easier way, rather than risking stepping so close to the edge of the cliff.

That being the case, she must have taken the more difficult ridge. She wouldn't have minded the challenge. She had more balls than most guys I knew. Or a cast iron pussy.

I turned towards the easier ridge and started to make my way carefully around the edge. Both ridges led to the same place, but this one would get me there more quickly. Taking the difficult route was unexpected, but it would, potentially, slow her down.

I kept my eyes and ears open. If this was the actual trials, it was exactly the kind of place I'd expect an ambush. That wasn't going to happen here, but it was treacherous nonetheless. The last thing I wanted was for me to end up at the bottom of a cliff. That would not help Lila to claim her throne. And it wouldn't end with me fucking her against a tree, or on the bare ground. Or…

I pushed the thought out of my mind for now. If I kept thinking like that, my heavy balls would drag me down. I needed my blood in the head on my shoulders, not the one in my pants.

"Focus, Hunt," I told myself. I pressed my lips together and kept moving.

The sound of snapping branches and grunting from behind me told me my brother was on the same ridge, making his way as loudly as he could. It wasn't laziness or carelessness on his part. No, there was strategy in everything we both did, including this. The amount of noise he was making was his way of trying to psych me out. If I knew where he was, I'd know he was close. He'd expect me to freak out and make mistakes.

Fuck that. I had no intention of doing either of those things. I moved carefully and kept my head as clear as possible, ignoring the sounds from behind me. And trying to ignore the frustration at not knowing where Slade was.

Was he so far behind us I wouldn't hear him anyway? That was possible, but for some reason I knew that wasn't the case. From past experience, I knew to rely on my instincts. They'd never let me down yet. Doing otherwise would get me killed. Or worse, I'd lose.

That wasn't going to happen.

"Ouch!" Parker cried out behind me. "Fucking tree." A branch cracked off and flew through the air.

It sailed over the side of the cliff and disappeared. A thud followed a moment later.

I grinned. Only Parker would stop to take vengeance on a branch at a time like this. He wasn't acting out of anger though, not really. He knew better than to get pissed off with inanimate objects. This was just another trick to remind me he was right on my heels. To make me stop and look back.

Keeping as silent as I could, I swept my gaze back and forth, looking for signs of Lila or Slade. She couldn't be that far ahead now. I stepped off the ridge and headed back east. I knew I closed the distance between us, but by how far? Was it enough to catch her before Slade did? Where was the slippery moth-erfucker anyway?

And where was Lila?

I caught a glimpse of movement up ahead. Just a flash. I stopped mid-step and watched, but I didn't see anything more.

I held my breath. Wait, there it was again. Some-thing dark moving slowly through the trees. I couldn't tell if it was Lila or Slade. It wasn't both of them, because there were no groans of pleasure yet. Good, he hadn't caught up to her.

I stepped carefully in the direction of the move-ment, keeping eyes and ears open. If that was Lila, Slade might not be far behind. If it was Slade, I didn't want to catch up to him, in case he decided to pull something. Even though we weren't officially competing, that didn't mean he wouldn't try to psych me out, or slow me down the way Parker was.

I was so busy looking ahead of me, I almost missed the trap in the ground in front of me. A hole carved out by nature, but covered by a person. Presumably left here from the last trial. Maybe to catch Parker and I out. Judging by the dry branches scattered haphazardly across the top of the hole, they were here for a while. Definitely not placed there by someone in advance of this year's trial.

I stepped around the hole, but stopped to crouch down beside it. I peeled off a couple of branches and peered inside.

It was empty. I half expected it to be full of bones from missing students. Every few years or so, one or two would go missing during the trials. The Academy would send out search parties and sniffer dogs, but once in a while they never turned up. I wouldn't like to be on the school board and have to explain that to their parents. Some may insist on the Academy being shut down. Having their children die was one thing, going missing was another.

Whatever, either way the Academy remained open and the trials continued.

I placed the branches back over the hole and

stood. If Parker was dumb enough to fall in, he could stay there until I was finished with Lila. Or until he got himself out. The hole was deep enough to break a bone on landing, and the sides were difficult to climb, but a few hours in there wouldn't kill him.

I stepped away carefully, trying to leave no sign I was right there. Parker might be trying to pretend to be the proverbial bull in a china shop, but he wasn't stupid. He knew as well as I did how to look for signs of people passing this way.

We practised before the trials in a bunch of different places. We followed people and had people follow us. We worked through a bunch of different scenarios, some of which were useful on the day. Others not, but they'd come in useful since. It never hurt to add to my skill set.

"Fuck," Parker growled. That was followed by a soft thud and a groan that sounded like he pulled himself back to his feet. I guessed he tripped, but didn't fall through the trap. Not yet anyway.

I smiled to myself as he let out a string of curses before staggering on.

In the corner of my eye, I saw another flash of movement. Closer now. I was almost certain it was Lila. She was so close I could almost taste her. Could almost hear her heart beating as she pushed her way through the trees, trying to keep ahead of us. The

112

sweat would be slick on her body like it was on mine. When I caught her, our skin would slide against each other, slapping wet when I thrust.

I slipped through the trees like a fox, weaving my way through and trying not to make a sound.

There it was again, movement. A flash of long dark hair, tied back in a ponytail.

The finishing line wasn't far ahead either. We made it sound vague, but she'd know when she reached it. That was the point. Everyone who undertook the trials would start to wonder how they were supposed to know when they ended. That little bit of fear, the paranoia, was yet another layer to the challenge.

She slowed to walk around some wattle bushes that grew up in her path.

I smiled to myself and went the other way. I slipped in between two trees and waited.

She cursed under her breath as she reached the boulders I knew she'd find. When she turned around and headed back to go the other way around the wattles, I was waiting for her.

"Caught you."

I spoke at the same time as Slade.

CHAPTER 12

HUNTER

I stared at him.

"What the fuck, dude? Where did you come from?" I caught up to Lila and grabbed her arm. She and Slade looked at me like I should know the answer.

"Oh, hey… What?" Parker caught up to us. "How-inhell? Slade started after us."

"Yeah, he was just about to explain." I didn't take my eyes off Slade.

The asshole grinned and jerked his head back behind him. "I drove. The rules were to catch Lila before she got to the road. No one ever said how." He looked even more smug than Parker after we disposed of Scott. Or anyone else we ever killed, for that matter. Rolled into one.

My gaze went from Slade to Lila. "You're not surprised."

I half expected her to encourage us to find a nice shallow grave for him. For her, I'd be happy to oblige.

"I figured he'd do something to get ahead of you two," she said with a smile. "How better than to jump back into the SUV?" She actually seemed impressed by his cheating ass.

I shoved down my annoyance to a place I could get at it later. No doubt it would come in useful. It always did.

I shrugged as though I didn't give a shit. "I still won. I caught Lila." I pulled her over to me. I was hard as hell. Even when I was annoyed, my cock didn't let me down. Right now, all he wanted was to be buried deep inside her.

"Actually, it was a tie," Slade said. "But I don't mind sharing." He stepped over to her and slid his hands up the back of her shirt.

"Crap," Parker grumbled.

"You're welcome to watch," I said over my shoulder.

"I was planning on it." Parker flopped down under a tree and pulled a packet of salted nuts out of his pocket. "I should have brought some beers too."

I laughed and gripped the front of Lila's shirt. I

ripped the front of it apart, sending buttons flying. It wouldn't be primal if I didn't literally tear the clothes off her body. I shoved what was left down her arms.

Slade grabbed it before it could fall to the ground.

He unhooked Lila's bra and pushed it off. The black lace slid to the ground and lay splayed apart. Slade grabbed her wrists and pulled them behind her. He wound her shirt around her wrists and tied it firmly. "Wouldn't want you running away again."

She gave us both a look, then twisted away from us and started to run through the trees.

I glanced at Slade and grinned. If that was how she wanted to play it, I was here for it.

He grinned back and we gave chase.

Running as awkwardly as she was, it didn't take us long to catch up to her again.

Slade grabbed her arm and yanked her back so hard he almost pulled her off her feet.

She fell back against him, giving me time to undo the top of her jeans and drag them down her legs. She kicked out at me, but I grabbed her ankle and pulled off one of her boots.

"Hold her." I dropped her foot and grabbed the other.

Slade wrapped his arms around her upper body and gripped her while she squirmed and fought.

I pulled off the other boot and tossed it aside before tugging her jeans the rest of the way off.

I smiled at her briefly before tearing her panties off.

"Open up." I pressed her panties against her lips.

She shook her head until I gripped her chin and forced her mouth open. I shoved her panties inside and slipped my hand between her legs.

"As I suspected, she's drenched." I shoved her legs apart and slipped a couple of fingers inside her. She wriggled and growled, but I knew she was enjoying every minute.

I slipped my fingers out long enough to undo my jeans, my grateful erection rock hard in my hand. I gripped the back of one one of Lila's thighs and Slade gripped the other. Between us we lifted her high enough to slide her onto my cock.

She wriggled and writhed, but the moment I was seated deep inside her, her eyes shone with excitement and pleasure.

"That's my girl. Always ready to take me." She felt so fucking good.

I gripped her hips so tight I knew I would leave bruises, and slid out of her. I slammed back in so hard she let out a cry of pain. That sound made my balls heavier than ever. I slammed into her again, harder than before. Again and again until tears poured from her eyes.

She rolled her hips to meet me. Her head tipped back, eyes closed before she came around my cock, clenching me so tight she forced an orgasm out of me. My balls contracted, exploding my cum inside her. I pumped and went on pumping until every drop was milked dry.

I sagged forward and stood for a few minutes before sliding out of her and lowering her legs to the ground.

Slade pulled the panties out of her mouth and pushed her down to her knees. He already had his cock out, but now he pressed it between her lips.

I grabbed a fistful of her hair and tugged her back, before guiding her forward until she was gagging on him. Over and over I shoved her on to him while he bucked, fucking her mouth hard.

"Fucking hell, her mouth," Slade said with a grunt.

"It's something else isn't it?" I agreed. Every time she gagged, Slade drew closer to the edge. "That's it, babe. Take him all the way down your pretty little throat. He's going to come in your mouth and you're going to swallow down every bit of it. Every drop."

In the corner of my eye, I caught Parker, cock in

his hand. His eyes were half closed, blissed out but watching. He looked close to coming too.

Slade went still, hands in fists at his sides. He pressed himself in deeper still before groaning long and low as he came.

Lila gagged again and swallowed hard a couple of times. By the time Slade slid out of her mouth, she was gasping for breath.

I kept my fingers tangled in her hair and let her recover before helping her to her feet.

"I'm guessing if I get caught during the trials it won't be that much fun." She stood still while Slade untied her shirt from her wrists.

"If it goes anything like that, I will be killing people," I said. If anyone touched a hair on her head against her will I'd strangle them with my bare hands. After slicing them to bits.

"We'll make sure they won't," Slade said. He slipped what was left of her shirt around her shoulders.

I tucked my cock back into my jeans and did them up.

"You did so well," I told her. "The road is only a few metres away." I nodded in that direction.

She turned to see the SUV parked under some trees beside the road.

"That didn't seem so difficult." She pulled the sides of her shirt tighter around herself.

"With only us chasing you it won't be," I agreed. "The actual trials will be different." I rubbed my chin and draped an arm around her shoulders. "I'm sure everyone would agree this was much more fun."

"Speak for yourself." Parker was tucking his cock back into his pants. "It could have been a bit more fun for me."

I grinned. "I guess you'll have to try harder next time, bro. But next time, no one drives." My annoyance came back to the surface and I gave Slade a dark look. So it wasn't an official rule, but it was an unspoken one. Up until now. If he did it again, I'd come right down on his cheating ass. Teacher or no teacher.

"No flying or anything else like that either," I added. I wouldn't put it past Parker to organise a helicopter if I didn't make the rules clear.

Although, now I thought about it, maybe I should have kept my mouth shut and done just that. I could have had Lila all to myself. On the other hand, having someone else hold her down added another layer of excitement to the chase. Just thinking about the way she struggled made my cock harden again.

I'd always had a thing for being dominant, but if she'd consent to a little role-play, I'd be a hundred percent there for it. The other guys too, by the look of them.

Without giving her any warning I was about to do it, I scooped Lila up and started towards the road. "One of you grab her jeans and boots," I called out over my shoulder.

She squealed in surprise, but then nestled into me, her arms around my neck.

"You enjoyed that?" I asked.

"More than I thought I would," she admitted. "Is that…weird? The way both of you were holding me and making me do what you wanted? It was… It was hot. I liked relinquishing control, but at the same time…" She thought as I stepped carefully over a fallen tree.

"At the same time, I was in control. I knew you would have understood if I said banana, even with my mouth full. You would have known if I really wanted you to stop. And you would have stopped. Both of you."

"Yes we would," I agreed. Stopping would have been difficult, and my balls would have hurt, but I would have backed right off. There was nothing in this world I wanted less than to hurt her. That would be like hurting the best piece of myself.

"I felt powerful, because I could let go and enjoy what you were doing. I didn't feel like the victim. Is that wrong? I mean… You were forceful." She looked up at me tentatively. Lila Bell was such a tough badass on the outside, but on the inside she had places that weren't broken. Places that were still soft, still sweet. Most people never saw that side of her. That I did right now was a testament to her feelings for me. We never spoke about it, but we both knew it for what it was. The woman held my heart in a vice, and I couldn't be happier.

"Nothing you could ever do would be wrong," I assured her. "There's no shame in wanting to be dominated once in a while. Or all the time. As long as you know you're the one calling the shots, there's no harm in it. If anything, it says how much you trust me and Slade. How many people do we know that we can really let go around and know they won't screw us over?"

"I know three," she said. "And all of them are right here."

"Is it Slade, me and yourself?" Parker asked jokingly.

"Fuck off," I told him. "If she's including herself, and she should, that makes four. If she's not, then clearly she meant herself, Slade and me."

"I meant you, Parker and Slade, dickhead," Lila told me. "But you're right, I should include myself. If I can't trust myself, then who will?"

"I will." I trusted this woman more than I trusted myself. If she told me the sky was pink, then it probably was. If she said I needed to kill someone for her, then I did. There was nothing I wouldn't do or say for her.

I turned sideways to the SUV and opened the door before placing her on the back seat. Before I could blink, Parker was around the other side and all but throwing himself in beside her.

He draped her jeans over her lap. "I couldn't find your panties. You won't need them for the ride home anyway." He grabbed her legs and turned her to face him, before opening her thighs and pressing his face between them.

I closed the door behind them and slipped into the front passenger seat. Just because he hadn't won didn't mean she shouldn't miss out on an orgasm or two on the drive back to the Academy.

I watched out the window as Slade drove and Lila groaned in the back seat. We didn't say a word most of the way, but that gave me time to think.

CHAPTER 13
LILA

I slipped my headphones off my ears and frowned.

When the knock came at the door again, I knew I wasn't hearing things. I also knew it wasn't Hunter or Parker, because they'd made their own keys and let themselves in when they felt like it. I should be annoyed at them, but I couldn't bring myself to be. Not even when I woke in the middle of the night with one of their cocks inside me.

I set the headphones aside and closed my laptop.

I rolled off the bed and unlocked the door. I opened it a crack and peered out.

I blinked in surprise.

"Zachary? What are you doing here?" I opened the door wider to let my former stepbrother in. He was tall and dark, with blue eyes that reminded me I definitely had a type. The attraction didn't go beyond the physical though.

I liked him, but there was no chance of us hooking up again. Certainly no chance of a relationship. That didn't mean I wasn't happy to see him. I was, it was just strange for him to drop in unannounced. Honestly, it was strange for anyone to drop in to Brutham unannounced. The Academy was tucked away from any major city and we weren't even close to the beach.

"Can I not pay my favourite stepsister a visit?" He kissed my cheek and stepped into the room. "Nice place."

I closed the door behind him. "It's no harbourside mansion, but it's all right," I said. "It's only for another couple of years." The rooms here were comfortable, but half the size of my room at home.

"Yeah, I guess so. I brought you something." He drew his hand out from behind his back and handed me a gift wrapped package. The paper was black, red and gold. My favourite combination. It was sweet of him to remember.

He sat in a chair while I flopped down on my bed and placed the package in my lap.

"You didn't have to get me anything." I pressed my hands into the sides of the parcel, like it was Christmas Day. My fingers sank into something soft.

"Of course I didn't, but I felt like it." He shrugged.

"This is the only reason you are here?" Call me cynical, but it was difficult not to find an ulterior motive wherever I looked. The whole competition between Chloe and I, and the trials at the end of the year, had me jumping at shadows. I knew well enough to know shadows were often more than shadows.

Without answering the question, he nodded towards the package. "Open it."

He crossed his legs, propping his ankle on his opposite thigh. He had the pose of a future master of the universe down pat. Then again, he'd been practising all his life the same way I had. My father was still one of his role models, although they weren't legally family anymore.

I looked down at the parcel. "It doesn't seem to be ticking."

Zachary chuckled.

Chloe would have peeled back the tape carefully, trying not to damage the paper.

Personally, I could never understand the point of having that kind of patience. I grabbed the slides and yanked them apart, tearing the paper down the middle.

Inside was a teddy bear the size of my arm, from my elbow to the tips of my fingers. He wore black trousers, red shirt, gold suspenders and a black, red and gold bowtie. His smiling face looked up at me, begging to be cuddled.

"He's so cute." I drew out the last word. I picked up the plush toy and wrapped my arms around him.

Zachary grinned. "The moment I saw him, I thought of you. I know you like those colours and you're probably homesick. Teddy bears make everything better, especially homesickness. I'm assuming here, because I've never had a teddy bear in my life." He wiggled his brows slightly.

"That is such a lie," I said with a laugh. "I remember Mr Snuggles. And that huge purple elephant you used to have. And the plush cockatoo. And—"

He raised his hands in surrender. "Okay, okay. You caught me. I'm a sucker for soft, squishy animals. Especially brightly coloured ones. Happy now?"

"I'll be happy when you admit to sleeping next to one of them," I said slyly.

He dropped his hands, letting them slap on his thighs. "I will never admit something like that. Anyway, I prefer my soft, squishy bed mates to be alive. And human," he added quickly when he saw me about to suggest he fucked animals.

I wrinkled my nose. "I don't think I want to hear

about your bed mates. There are things a girl doesn't want to know about her brother." I would always see him that way, regardless of what happened between my father and his mother. That was their business. My relationship with Zachary was mine.

"Shame, because the details are juicy." He grinned.

I pulled a face. "I'll take your word for it." I doubt he wanted to hear about my sex life any more than I wanted to hear about his.

"Does he have a name?" I nodded down at the teddy bear to change the subject.

"You'd trust someone who calls his bear Mr Snuggles to name yours?" Zachary gave me a lopsided smile.

"Good point," I said. "If it was up to me, I'd name him Ted E Bear."

"In that case, let me think of something. How about Reginald?"

I snorted a laugh. "I'm not calling a teddy bear Reginald."

"Fine," Zachary drawled. "How about Francisco? Laurence? I know, Terence. You could call him Terry Bear."

I aimed a kick at the front of his leg, even though I was too far away to reach. "I swear, these suggestions are getting worse."

"You try then." He lifted his chin in challenge.

"What would you call him, Brantley?" Something flickered in his eyes, but it was gone before I could pin down what it was.

"It's a better name than Terry Bear." I could just picture the expression on my father's face if I named the plush that.

He'd be only slightly less horrified than he would knowing I was still with Hunter and Parker. Some day that penny would drop and I was dreading it. That revelation had to wait until after my father chose me to head the family. Otherwise, he may choose Chloe instead.

I was almost certain the only reason she hadn't told him was because she was screwing a DiMarco. In the eyes of my father, that would be just as bad. He probably had some ally of his lined up to marry me, but that wasn't going to happen. Not if I could help it.

"I think I'll name him Herman," I said finally. That was cute and wouldn't raise any eyebrows or cause any trouble.

"Herman it is then," Zachary said. He glanced down and I knew he was finally ready to talk about what he'd really come here for.

I waited.

He looked back up. "I heard about your father pitting you and Chloe against each other. Herman is kind of a peace offering. Before you say anything, I got one for Chloe too. I have no intention of coming between you two, or taking sides one way or another."

"Do you wish he chose you?" I asked gently.

Zachary was older than Chloe and me, and male. If he was dad's biological son, he would have been the logical choice. Chloe and I would have been put to good use on behalf of the family, in some capacity or other. Whether that meant being married off or trained to work in some particular arm of the business, I didn't know. Maybe both.

There was a time when I thought Dad might insist Chloe or I marry Zachary. Then he could legitimately hand the business over to him and whichever one of us he married. But as time went by, the possibility became less and less likely. Just as well, I didn't want to hurt Zachary by refusing. There was no way Hunter, Parker and Slade would share me with him as well. Even if I was inclined to ask them to, which I wasn't.

"Sam would never have chosen me," Zachary said. "Even if he and Mum were still together, I'm only the step kid."

"Dad loves you," I argued. "So do I. You're not *only* anything. You're Zachary Sinclair. You're a card-carrying badass, motherfucker."

His smile was brief. "Literally. But I'm not a Bell. That makes all the difference."

I sat Herman aside and moved over to sit in the seat beside Zachary. I took his hand.

"I'm sorry if anyone made you feel like you're not enough. Who do I need to kill? Don't say my father, that would make all sorts of things more complicated."

His smile was more genuine now, the bitter edge dulled. "If anyone else asked that, I'd think they were joking. Not you though. You'd totally go out there and stab someone for your family." He made a repeated stabbing motion with his other hand.

"Yes, I would." I gave him a short nod. "Or better yet, I'd send someone to do it. Blood is a bitch to get out of clothes. Actually, when it comes down to it, poison is a lot less messy."

It was slower and more satisfying to watch the victim's eyes bug out and their face swell. They knew what was going to happen and were powerless to stop it. If they did something so terrible to warrant the poison, they deserved every moment of what they got.

"Will you give me a job when you're head of the family?" Zacahry asked, tugging my thoughts back to the present. "I know I won't be a Brutham graduate, but I have some useful skills. You know I'm good with my tongue." He grinned.

"Yes you are, and yes you do," I agreed. It would be better if I didn't think too much about his tongue. That was the past and we wouldn't revisit it again.

"I'd be more than happy to give you a job. Hell, I'd give Chloe a job if she stepped aside now and agreed never to undermine me." Which I knew full well she would never agree to. That was probably just as well too, because I didn't think I'd ever be able to trust her again.

"Is that why you came here, to ask for a job?" I teased. "I'm sure you have prospective bosses lining up at your door to hire you." Why wouldn't they? He was intelligent, resourceful and charming. He'd be an asset to any business, including mine.

"You'd think so, wouldn't you? Maybe there are, but I know who I want to work for. Besides, the Bell's have better perks than anywhere else."

"We're slightly less inclined to get angry if you kill a coworker?" I only half joked.

While that did occasionally happen, they had to have a very good reason for doing it, like the person they killed was stealing from the company, or betrayed us somehow. If you killed someone who looked at you the wrong way, you'd end up in a shallow grave beside them. Neither my father nor I had time for any of that bullshit.

"Exactly," Zachary agreed. "Anyway, I've kept you long enough. I should be getting back to Sydney. I have an exam in the morning." He grimaced.

I matched his expression. "Me too." The only reason the guys weren't here was because we were all studying for exams, and they distracted me too much. If they had their way, they'd be chasing me through the forest in the dark, rather than letting me study. While I preferred their idea, I couldn't afford not to do well. Chasing would have to wait.

When he stood, I stood with him and gave him a hug.

"Thank you for coming. And for Herman. It's been good to see you." I kissed his cheek.

"You too." He kissed mine back. "Herman will help you to sleep well tonight. Have sweet dreams. Goodbye."

His words lingered in my mind long after he slipped out the door, but I put them out of my mind and got ready for bed.

CHAPTER 14

HUNTER

"Are you sure about this?" Parker asked. "She has an exam in a few hours. You know how she gets when she's woken up before an exam."

His face was still sleepy from falling asleep on my bed while we studied for our exam. I tried to sneak out without waking him, but of course he heard me. Nothing I could say would persuade him to stay and go back to sleep. I considered handcuffing him to my bed, but it was too much of a hassle, and my cock needed to see Lila.

I flashed him a grin. "That's half the fun. She gets pissed off with us and we get to make it up to her." I pulled the key out of my pocket.

"Wait." He caught my wrist before I could put the key in the lock. "What is that?"

I was halfway to assuming it was some kind of

joke. An attempt to shove me out of the way and get in first.

A moment later, I caught his tone and froze. My gaze dropped to the base of the door.

Wisps of something white drifted out from the gap at the bottom.

"Fuck." I shoved the key into the lock frantically and pushed the door open. We both almost tumbled inside. I staggered a step or two and caught a whiff.

The smell wafted through the corridor. How had I not noticed it until now? It was sickly sweet and slightly nauseating. My eyes watered and my nose started to run.

"That's not smoke." I grabbed the bottom of my shirt with one hand and pulled it off over my head. I pressed it against my mouth and hurried into Lila's room.

The fumes were thicker here. Not as thick as smoke, but thick enough to be visible. And to sting my skin and eyes. I wiped away tears and blinked several times to clear them.

"Shit."

Lila lay on her bed like she was asleep, hair fanned out across her pillow. Her long lashes lay against her cheeks. Her lips were parted slightly. Her skin was pale as death.

Something lay on the bed beside her, fumes

winding their way toward the ceiling. It looked like a teddy bear.

What the fuck?

"Don't breathe it in," I told my twin. I coughed a couple of times into the cotton of my shirt. The fumes coated my lungs, making it harder to breathe.

"We need to get her out of here." I tied the arms of my shirt around the back of my head to keep it in place and scooped her up. I'd be no use to her if I inhaled too much of the stuff and passed out. If that happened, we'd all be screwed.

"What the fuck?" Parker stood staring at the teddy bear. "Wild guess, we need to get this out of here too." He threw the bed covers over the teddy bear to cut off the gas, gathered it up tight and carried it out of the room behind us.

"Be careful of that thing. I'm guessing it's some kind of nerve agent. We need to get her to the Academy hospital."

She was limp in my arms, barely breathing. If she died, whoever left that fucking teddy bear would regret the day they were born. Fuck it, when she made a complete recovery I'd still make sure they regretted the day they were born. No one messes with my queen and gets away with it.

"What do we do with this thing?" Parker was holding the covers firm around the teddy bear, his own shirt pressed against his face. He looked as angry as I was. Between us, we'd rip whoever did this to Lila, to shreds.

"We need to bring it with us," I said. "The sooner they know what it is, the sooner they can treat her." For the first time, I regretted studying cyber security. If I'd studied medicine or chemistry, I may have some idea of how to fix this. If she wasn't all right...

I pushed the thought away and trotted through the corridor. I couldn't let myself think that way. She'd be fine. She had to be. My heart would shatter irreparably if she wasn't. The pieces left would be smaller than grains of sand. A Brantley with a broken heart was the definition of dangerous. I'd end worlds if she didn't recover.

I turned around and pushed the hospital door open with my back.

"I need help!" I shouted. I didn't care who else was in here and what injuries they might have. Lila was my priority. The only priority. Everyone else could fucking wait.

A nurse immediately sprang to her feet and hurried out from behind the long wooden desk. "Bring her through." She waved towards a door to the side of the room and pressed a button on the wall. "The doctor won't be long."

"By *not long* you better mean no more than a

minute," I snarled. I'd grab a scalpel and make the doctor treat her right now if I had to. I didn't give a fuck if someone else was dying in another part of the hospital.

I carried Lila through into the examining room and gently laid her down on the narrow bed in the centre. She looked so small and vulnerable lying there. Like a doll at the mercy of a child with a pair of scissors, or one who liked to remove the heads from their toys to swap them around.

She would have hated seeing herself like this. If there was something she couldn't stand, it was being vulnerable. I hated it too, because it reminded me she was only human. Fragile.

I forced breaths in and out. I had to be calm. She didn't need me losing my shit now. If anyone could fix her, it was the medical staff here.

Like everything else here at Brutham, the hospital was the best money could buy. Better than the average infirmary. Better, if I was honest, than any other hospitals. It was rarely very busy and, lucky for them, was well staffed.

I tore the shirt off my face and tossed it aside.

"What's happened?" The doctor on duty's name was Racquel. In her mid-thirties, I knew her from previous injuries and several fucks before I met Lila.

When she hurried into the room, she was all business.

"Someone tried to poison her with some kind of gas from this." Parker held out the pile of covers.

Racquel nodded and stuck her face out the door. "Henry, come and take this. Figure out what was in it."

I didn't look up to see who Henry was. I didn't give a shit. All of my attention was on Lila and how shallow her breathing was. I leaned down and pressed my cheek to hers.

"You're going to be okay, babe. You're in the best hands here. They'll take care of you."

If I thought there was any better, I'd send a helicopter for them right now. But Brutham had the best doctors, all of them highly skilled and paid well to turn a blind eye to everything they saw here. If they ever wrote a book about their experiences, no one would believe it anyway. Not that they'd get to write it, because the Academy would never allow that.

Racquel started on all her doctor things, checking Lila's pulse and pupils. "Any idea how long she was like this?"

"We found her five minutes ago," Parker said. He moved to the other side of the bed. His arms were empty, his shirt gone from over his face. "No idea before that. Although, she usually goes to sleep around midnight."

Racquel glanced at the clock on the wall. "It's almost 3 AM. Potentially three hours. Probably less. If it was that long, it's unlikely she'd still be alive."

Fury burned a path through my body. If we hadn't snuck in, she'd be dead. Murdered by whoever left that fucking teddy bear.

When I found who did this, they'd regret the day their parents were born, nevermind themselves. Their death was going to be slow and very, very painful. I might play with them for a couple of weeks first. Make them beg to die.

"You both need to step back and give us room," Racquel barked. She ordered the nurse to bring over an oxygen mask and tank. In moments, the mask was over Lila's face, pumping the precious substance into her.

I stood back beside Parker. If they thought that would make us leave, they'd need to think again. We weren't leaving her side.

Parker pulled out his phone and sent off a text. "Slade," was all he said.

I nodded vaguely. All I cared about right now was Lila.

A man slipped into the room and said something

to Racquel before slipping back out. Something about chlorine and level two nerve agent.

Racquel grabbed a needle of something and tapped at it to get out the bubbles. She inserted it into a vein in Lila's arm and pressed the plunger.

"The next hour or two will be critical," she said, addressing everyone present. "Much longer and it would have been too late, but I'm confident she should make a full recovery."

"She better," Parker growled.

Racquel looked at him, unflinchingly. "It depends on her and how strong she is. She's young and fit, she should be fine. I can't guarantee there won't be long term side effects. The best you can do right now is focus on her recovery." She turned back to Lila, quickly assessing her progress.

I put my arm around Parker. "Lila is a badass bitch. She's too stubborn to be taken out by a fucking teddy bear."

"This was Chloe, wasn't it?" Parker gritted his teeth together, barely containing his anger. "We knew she'd do something, and she has. I'm going to rip her fucking face off. And that prick, Dane, while I'm at it. This was probably his idea. Motherfucking son of a whore's bitch."

Slade came barrelling into the room. He skidded to a stop right before he ran into us. He took one look at Lila and his face turned red. We didn't need to exchange words. We were all thinking the same thing. By the time we were done, there was going to be nothing left of any of Lila's enemies.

"This is fucked up." Parker didn't take his eyes off our queen. "If she dies—"

"She's not going to die," Slade said. "She has too much unfinished business to take care of. Too much life left to live."

But Lila looked so pale and helpless laying there, mask over her mouth and nose. Her eyelids twitched once in a while, and her chest rose and fell. If it wasn't for those and the machine monitoring her vitals, I would have thought she was dead.

Chloe won.

If she did, the bitch wouldn't win for long. Samuel Bell would lose both of his daughters. I didn't care that it would start a war between him and my family. Fuck the consequences. Chloe was going to pay for this.

"Has anyone informed her sister?" Racquel asked. "Or the rest of her family?"

"We are her family," Parker snapped. "We're the only family she needs."

"That may be so," Racquel said slowly, "but I'm obligated to inform her biological family."

"We'll tell them," I said. "They should know. Leave

it to us."

Racquel nodded and ducked out of the room.

Parker glanced at me. "What the hell? Chloe doesn't deserve—"

I interrupted him. "Look at Lila. She's alive. Don't you want to see the expression on Chloe's face when she finds out she failed? When she realises we know she's behind this and that we're going to come after her for it?"

His mouth turned up in a slow, humourless smile. "Yeah, I do want to see that. Slade?"

"I'll stay here with Lila." He pulled a chair over to the bed and sat before taking Lila's hand in his.

"We won't be long." I gave her a long look. For the first time, I seriously considered suggesting Lila concede the role of head of the family. Let Chloe have it. Then, when the time was right, we'd destroy everything Samuel Bell built and bring Chloe to her knees. Was it worth putting Lila at risk anymore? If Chloe did this, then hell only knows what else she might pull.

Fucking with her birth control was one thing, but this was war. One I was determined to win, no matter how dirty we had to play to win it. If she really thought screwing with us was a good idea, she was wrong.

So, so fucking wrong.

CHAPTER 15

LILA

I woke to the sound of whooshing and soft beeping. Something was on my face. I moved my head from side to side slowly, but couldn't dislodge it. Panic started to rise. The beeping increased in speed.

What the absolute fuck?

"Hey, Lila. It's okay. Calm down. It's just an oxygen mask."

Who was that? My sleepy mind took a while to register who it was. Slade.

Oxygen mask? What the hell?

I opened my eyes a crack, closed them again immediately. The glare was too much.

"Lila, I need you to open your eyes," a female voice said. "I need to look at your pupils."

"Do what the doctor says," Slade ordered. "Open your eyes."

I tried to tell him to fuck off, but the mask and my sluggish brain wouldn't let the words come.

I opened my eyes again and winced at the glare of a torch shining into them.

I wanted to tell the doctor to fuck off too.

"Good. You're doing well. Let the oxygen breathe for you for a while longer. We should be able to take the mask off soon." She turned the torch off and the room went darker.

"Is she going to be okay?" That was Parker's voice. He sounded worried, tense. People should get out of his and Hunter's way when they were like that. Someone was likely to die if they looked at them wrong. Why was he worried though? What happened?

"It's too early to tell, but the signs are positive," the doctor said.

"She'll be all right," Hunter snapped. His face appeared above me. He looked tired. His eyes were red. "Right, babe?"

All I could do was look back at him and make a sound in the back of my throat. I regretted that immediately. My throat was dry, like someone had run sandpaper up and down the inside of it.

"Let her get some rest," the doctor said. "I'll be back in an hour. Hopefully she won't need the oxygen then and we can see if she's up to eating. The rest of you should get some breakfast."

Breakfast? How long was I asleep? Fuck, I had an exam this morning. What time was it anyway?

The beeping increased speed again.

"It's okay, babe." Hunter took my hand. "Don't worry about anything except getting better. Relax. We've got you, I promise."

I forced myself to relax, if only because the doctor might sedate me if I didn't. I hated the idea of being given drugs because I couldn't control myself properly. That wasn't me. I was Lila Bell. I was the one in full control.

Me.

The beeping slowed.

"Funny story," Hunter said. "I went and told Chloe you were still alive. She tried to pretend she had no idea what was going on, but I knew she was full of shit. She definitely knew who put that teddy bear in your room."

I blinked hard. Teddy bear?

Herman.

Zachary.

Zachary did this to me? My head spun with the implications of that. I thought he cared about me. He came to me to say he wasn't getting involved…

He fucking lied. Everything he said was bullshit.

That whole time, he was there on Chloe's behalf. He was working with her or for her. The only thing he said that was honest was that the teddy bear would help me sleep. He meant it when he said goodbye.

He knew when he left that the bear contained a booby-trap meant to kill me.

No wonder Hunter thought the conversation with Chloe was funny. She must have been pissed when she learned she failed. She'd tried to kill me, but I survived. I was stronger than that. I'd make a full recovery and then I'd go after her.

"You know too, don't you?" Slade asked. "Someone was in your room?"

He looked ready to rip their arms off and strangle them with them. Teddy bear or no teddy bear, he was furious at the idea of someone being in my room and him not knowing about it.

Hunter looked equally unimpressed. He and Parker knew about Zachary, but neither of them were fans of my former stepbrother. When they found out what he did…

I managed to nod in spite of the mask.

"You can tell us as soon as the doctor lets you take that off," Parker said.

Hunter looked to the side.

"What? I can be the voice of reason once in a while," Parker protested. "The most important thing here is that Lila gets better. We can worry about revenge later."

"Right." Hunter looked back at me. "It will be sweeter after they've stewed for a while anyway. Let them think we aren't coming after them. When they least expect it." He grinned. "We'll fuck them so hard they'll wish they hadn't touched you."

He sounded like he was very much looking forward to doing just that. Hell had no fury like me and one of my guys when someone fucked with us.

"Didn't you two say something about having exams?" Slade asked. "Go and get something to eat and get them done. You're not going to help Lila if you fail."

He stepped over to the other side of me and brushed hair back off my forehead. "Don't worry about yours, you can take it when you're better."

"Don't you have a class to teach?" Hunter asked.

"Not until after lunch," Slade replied. "I'll stay with Lila until then."

Both twins hesitated before Hunter nodded. "We'll be back as soon as the exam is over." He leaned over and kissed my cheek.

Parker shoved him out of the way and did the same.

I turned my head to watch them step out of the room.

"You're safe with me," Slade said softly.

I held his gaze. I wanted to believe him. I *did* believe him, but I believed the same of Zachary. Now, I realised how naïve that was. It never crossed my mind he might do anything like this to me.

I trusted him.

I trusted him and he tried to kill me. All this time he was on Chloe's side and I didn't have a clue. Did Dane know? How could he not?

"We got lucky," Slade said. His expression was closed except for a hint of suppressed emotion in his eyes. He was also used to being in control of himself and those around him, to keeping himself guarded against the world. I suspected if he was with anyone else he wouldn't let it even slip this far.

I frowned at him.

"If the twins hadn't found you in time, we would have lost you. Yeah, we haven't known each other for long, but losing you would..." He cleared his throat.

"I suck at all this expressing emotion shit. I just wanted to say I'm fucking glad we didn't lose you. Not only because if we did, the twins would probably burn Brutham to the ground." A faint hint of a smile brushed his lips.

That was exactly what they'd do. With Chloe and Dane inside. They'd sit outside on the front lawn with beer and pizza, and watch. And laugh while my sister and her lover screamed.

No one would ever accuse them of being too sweet.

I gave Slade a questioning look.

"You're wondering what I would do?" He mused on that for a while. "I'd probably drive the getaway car, and be their alibi. I'd like to think I have enough credibility that if I say they were with me, I'd be believed. I might even help them spread accelerant all around the building before they lit a match."

He mimed striking a match against a matchbox and throwing it. Followed by his hands rising in the to signify fire, or an explosion.

His boyish smile made him look younger. Evidently, he had the same violent streak as the twins. I wondered if they were related somehow. Or maybe I just attracted sadistic men.

That suited me just fine.

Imagining the guys destroying the place shouldn't have been hot, but it was. All three of the guys would do more than burn the Academy down. They'd burn the whole world down for me. And then dance in the ashes. They'd get off on doing it.

"It won't come to that," Slade added. "We'll deal with this. We'll teach them they fucked with the wrong people. By the time we're done, they'll wish

Chloe hadn't relinquished everything to you. They'll wish she ran, dropped off the face of the earth while she could. But she didn't and that was her mistake. Like Hunter said, when we fuck back, we're going to fuck back hard."

He emphasised the last word with a nod, his nose slightly scrunched, teeth bared.

I closed my eyes and exhaled softly. I was tired, but more than that I was angry. At myself for letting Zachary in and accepting that present. For listening to his lies and not seeing them for what they were. For knowing there was meaning in what he said but not taking the time to think it through and realise something was up. For not realising he brought a Trojan horse to my door and welcoming it with open arms and even cuddles.

I even named the fucking thing. I was naïve and stupid and I could have died because of it.

I was angry at Chloe for being a spineless bitch. She couldn't even come at me herself, she had to send Zachary on her behalf. Even if he swore up and down this was her idea, she'd deny it. She'd go to the grave denying it.

Somewhere in the back of my mind, I was angry at my father too. Sure, Chloe did this, but this whole competition bullshit was his idea. He could have chosen one of us and been done with it.

Even as I was thinking that, I realised it wouldn't have been that simple. If he chose Chloe, I would have insisted he change his mind. If he chose me, she would have done the same. We would have resented each other and him until one of us was dead.

Maybe that was the idea. He wanted one of us to kill the other, because he was too gutless to do it. Too much of a coward to cut one of our throats. Instead, he pitted us against each other, forcing us to do his dirty work for him. Making us hate each other more and more, until our relationship was shredded into nothing.

I hoped he was satisfied, because that was exactly what was happening. If Chloe was in front of me right now, I'd wrap my hands around her throat and squeeze until her body went limp, her lips blue, her eyes lifeless.

I'd stare at the dead body that looked a lot like me and know I'd won.

The only thing I knew for certain right now was that I *would* win. This attack made me more determined than ever.

Creeping around in the shadows, sending Zachary with a teddy bear, that was unbecoming of the Bell family. Both of them should be ashamed of themselves.

Zachary was right, he wasn't a Bell; he never

would be. He didn't have what it took. Neither of them did.

I would head the family with Hunter, Parker and Slade by my side. And the whole fucking world would tremble.

CHAPTER 16
LILA

I dropped my books onto the top of the table with a thud that made Chloe jump. Smiling in satisfaction at her response, I flopped down in the chair opposite her. Arms on the table in front of me, I sat looking at her.

"You're up out of bed, I see," she said sweetly. It would be obvious to anyone listening that she wasn't only referring to the hospital.

I ignored her attempt to slut shame me —as if she could talk anyway—and smiled.

"Yes, I've made a full recovery. The doctor says I won't have any lingering side-effects." That was almost the truth. The doctor said she *thought* I wouldn't, but I may suffer problems in the future.

In the short term, I tired more quickly, but that would pass.

"That's wonderful," Chloe said, as if she wasn't seething on the inside. "I'm so relieved. I was worried about you. I popped in to visit, but you'd already been discharged. I figured you'd be resting."

You're full of shit, I thought.

"Always so thoughtful," I said sarcastically. "Where did you get the teddy bear from?" I was done tiptoeing around the truth. We both knew I knew exactly what happened. The only reason I didn't jump over the table right now and strangle her was because there were witnesses. That and I wanted her to suffer.

"Zachary gave it to me," she said with mock innocence. "She's so cute, with her little blue tutu." She cocked her head. "What's wrong? He didn't give you one too?" She clicked her tongue in mock sympathy.

"You know he did," I snapped. "Inside it was a capsule of toxic gas and a timer to release it. Which you know all about, because it was your idea. Yours or his. How long have you been working together?" I hadn't meant to ask that. I didn't want to talk about Zachary, but the words were out and I wanted the answer anyway. Not that I was naïve enough to think she'd give me one.

"I have no idea what you're going on about. Why would Zachary work with me?" She laughed, but the sound was higher than usual, as it was when she was nervous.

I rested my elbows on the table and clasped my hands in front of me. The black gloss polish on my nails caught the light.

"I've been asking myself the same question. The only answer I can come up with is a momentary lapse of judgement on his part. Or maybe he *wanted* to be on the losing side. Why—I assume it involves you sucking his cock."

Chloe leaned forward, resting her own elbows on the table. Her own nails were baby pink.

"Has it crossed your mind I had nothing to do with what happened? Have you, even for a second, considered he was working alone? You should be flattered. Out of both of us, he went after you. He could just as easily have tried to kill me too. Then what would have happened? Dad would have had no choice but to make Zachary his heir."

"Dad would choose Kennedy before he chose Zachary," I said. Our older half sister had already renounced any claim on any part of the family inheritance, but if we were gone, Dad would find a way to convince her to change her mind. He could be persuasive when he needed to be.

"Then perhaps you should warn Kennedy that Zachary might come after her." Chloe shrugged.

"He won't go after her if he didn't go after you," I said. "And the only reason he didn't go after you was because you and he are working together. By your own reasoning, he has no reason to leave you alive."

"Unless he thinks he can use me for something. Hell, for all I know my teddy bear has a capsule inside it that hasn't gone off yet." She sat back.

"Prove it," I said. "Show me this bear."

"Don't you have a make-up exam to study for?" she asked.

"After I see the bear." I couldn't entirely discount the possibility Zachary did this all by himself. Getting rid of us and Kennedy would force Dad's hand. Dad would be pissed if he killed us, but he'd appreciate Zachary's ambition.

Chloe sighed loudly. "Fine. Let's get this over with then. Some of us have work to do." She snatched up her books and laptop and stomped away.

I scooped up my own books and strode after her.

I hadn't been in her room since we first arrived at Brutham. I'd helped carry a couple of boxes from the car, but hadn't had a reason to be here after that.

Like our rooms at home, mine looked like a bomb went off inside a wardrobe. Clothes were always scattered all over the floor and on the top of the desk and chair. A bra often dangled over the edge of my bed.

Like always, Chloe's room was spotless. If I didn't know better, I'd think she didn't live here. The space was too tidy for a normal person.

"Here it is." She snatched up the teddy bear and all but threw it at me.

I grabbed it and squeezed its torso. "I need a knife."

"What makes you think I keep a knife here?" she asked, like cum wouldn't melt in her mouth.

I gave her a sidelong glance and held out my hand.

She rolled her eyes but stepped over to the table beside the bed and opened the drawer. She pulled out a knife and handed it to me, blade first.

I eyed her carefully, before taking the blade between my thumb and forefinger and slipping it out of her hand. I wouldn't put it past her to take this opportunity to stab me. I would have seriously considered it myself, but she didn't.

I moved a neat pile of books stacked on her desk, to the side and placed the teddy on the scratched, mahogany surface. I slashed the knife across the plush torso, exposing the stuffing. Placing the knife out of reach of my dear sister, I started to pull the stuffing out of the teddy bear.

I got halfway when something caught the overhead light. A glint of something shiny. Something familiar.

I glanced up at Chloe before digging my fingers in and pulling out a metal tube with a rounded end, like an elongated capsule. It was connected to a small, plastic device.

Her mouth dropped open. For the first time in I couldn't remember how long, she seemed genuinely surprised.

I won't lie, so was I.

"That fucking asshole," she growled. "He dared to come after me?"

"You didn't seem too worried when you thought it was just me he tried to kill," I said dryly.

She took the capsule for a closer look. "It's more personal when someone tries to kill you. Especially when you didn't realise *that* someone hates your guts."

For some reason, her words actually stung.

"I don't—" I started to say.

She glanced up at me. "You can't finish that sentence, can you?"

I pressed my lips together. "Chloe, I don't hate your guts. I hate this situation. I hate that in order to get the one thing I want in this world, I have to step over you."

She opened and closed her mouth a couple of times. "And now Zachary is trying to step over both of us."

"Yes, he is." We could agree on that at least.

"Are we going to let him do that?" She placed the capsule back inside the teddy bear and covered it with stuffing. "We should get rid of this before that goes off. I don't want to assume it failed. It might be on a different timer to yours."

I glanced around the room.

"Open the window."

She frowned at me. "I don't —"

"Open the window!" I didn't wait for her to move. I picked up a chair and slammed it straight into the glass. It cracked, but didn't break. Of course it didn't, the windows here were a couple of layers thick. Not quite bullet-proof, but close to it. Thank fuck they weren't bullet-proof, I'd never get through that. Not with a chair.

I pulled it back and slammed it into the window again. And again until finally a small section broke. It wasn't much, but it would have to do.

I grabbed up the whole teddy bear and shoved it through the hole. It dropped out and onto the ground below. Grabbing Chloe by the wrist, I pulled her down low to the floor. I threw myself down beside her, landing hard on my shoulder. I winced with pain but manage to throw my arms over my head.

"What the fuck—"

Her words were cut off by a bang loud enough to rattle the glass in the windows on the floor below this one. That was followed by a cloud of dust and smoke.

I lay with my face pressed to the hardwood. My heart pounded. My body was damp with sweat. I struggled to get my mind around what just happened.

When I was finally able to speak, I said, "Are you flattered now? He came after us both." I coughed lightly as smoke drifted in through the hole in the window.

Chloe choked on a laugh and managed to sit up. Her usually neat hair was in disarray, strands stuck out all over. She swept it back off her face. "How did you know?"

"I guessed," I admitted. "If there were cameras in your room, when would it be better to let off a bomb? He might have intended it just for you, but when the gas didn't kill me, he had to improvise. He could have taken us both out at the same time."

She looked disgusted. "This just got very, very fucking personal." She leaned her back against the side of her bed. I know we're supposed to be competing with each other, but he's pissed me off." She sucked in an angry breath.

"Why don't we call a truce until we deal with him? Otherwise, he's going to go on using our animosity towards each other, against us. I don't know about you, but I don't want to fight a war on two fronts. If we keep doing that, we both lose."

She offered me her hand.

I looked at it for a good minute before I finally accepted it and shook. "We can't let him take what's ours." Relinquishing control of the family to her would be difficult enough. Seeing Zachary running it wasn't something I could allow. Even if he was a Bell by blood, he'd done something I couldn't forgive. He'd tried to kill me, twice. That really, really pissed me off.

"No we can't." I scooted over and leaned against the bed beside her. "He's going to regret fucking with the wrong sisters."

I didn't know how long this tentative truce would last, but between us we'd fuck back against Zachary harder than we ever would have against each other. It might even feel good to be on the same side as her for a while.

"Yes he is. And you owe me an apology." She gave me a sly smile. "You thought I sent that bear."

I flipped her off. "For one thing, I had good reason to think that. If the tables were turned, you would have thought I attacked you. Also, I just saved your ass. I could have walked out the door, closed it behind me and let that bomb go off with you in the room."

"You wouldn't do that," she said. "Deep down, you love me. Besides, you couldn't know how powerful that bomb was. It could have taken out the corridor with you in it."

"You're right in the second count." I wasn't going to say anything about the first point. Maybe she was right. That wasn't something I needed to dwell on right now.

When Zachary was dealt with, we'd go back to being bitter enemies. I had no reason to assume otherwise. At this point, we'd been at each other's throats for so long, I didn't know if we could do any different.

She snorted softly. "There's something you should know."

"You're sleeping with Dane DiMarco, everyone knows that," I said lightly.

She rolled her eyes to the ceiling. "I don't care who knows that. Dane is—" She shook her head. "That doesn't matter at the moment. When Zachary was here, he told me he was transferring to Brutham.

They're going to make sure he does the trials along with us."

We exchanged knowing looks.

"That is interesting," I said slowly. "He may regret that choice."

"If he lives long enough to regret it," she said. "Personally, I'd be okay with him being long gone before that."

"So would I," I agreed. "Although…after what he did to us, I'd be just as happy to make him suffer for a while."

CHAPTER 17

HUNTER

"Or we could just rip his balls off and shove them down his throat." I bit into my apple like I might tear a piece off Zachary and spit it out.

Parker and I were in class when we heard the explosion outside the window. Although it was several metres from where we sat, the whole building shook. The windows rattled. The bomb left a crater the size of my outstretched arms in the manicured lawn. Small in the scheme of things, but big enough to kill Lila and her sister if it went off in the same room as them.

Needless to say, I was pissed off. Coming after Lila once was bad enough. Twice was a one way trip to the perpetrator's worst nightmare. That was a ticket I was happy to spring for.

Sitting opposite Chloe and Dane, on the same side

for once, was as surreal as it was temporary. I trusted them as much as I trusted Zachary, but if Lila said they were working together, then I'd play nice.

For now.

"I'm not ruling that out," Lila said. "I don't want to kill him outright just yet."

"Why?" Parker asked. "You'd be surprised how many problems can be solved by killing someone outright."

"I hate to say it, but Parker is right," Dane said. He sat beside Chloe, his arm draped across the back of the couch behind her. He was tense. Ready to defend her if any of us made a move.

Parker grinned. "Thanks, dude. I keep telling Hunter that but he thinks I'm biased."

"I didn't say you were biased," I argued. "I said you were full of shit. There's a significant difference."

He flipped me off. "I love you too, bro."

"Anyway," Dane drawled. "This asshole tried to kill both of you and you don't want him dead?"

"Oh, we want him dead all right," Lila said. "But we want to toy with him first. Make an example of him. Killing him would be too easy. We want this to be memorable."

"Exactly," Chloe agreed. "We want people to know what happens when they fuck with the Bell family. We want what we do to him to serve as a deterrent to anyone else who thinks we're pushovers because we're women."

"The only people who think that are people who haven't met you," Slade said. He sat quietly in the corner until now. Watching and listening, his eyes following the conversation back and forth across the room.

"See, Slade is all for killing Zachary and getting it over with," Parker said.

Slade raised his eyebrows. "On the contrary, if this helps to deter other people from causing problems later, then I'm all for playing cat and mouse with Zachary. Although six of us against one of him... I almost feel sorry for the asshole."

"Don't," Lila told him. "There's nothing to feel sorry for him for. He made his bed and now he has to lie in it."

She lifted her chin, her dark eyes darker than ever. She was absolutely fucking gorgeous and glorious. She was the flame and I was one of the moths drawn to her heat and light, not caring if I got burnt to a crisp. I couldn't think of a better way to go.

"Why would he come here?" I asked. "He failed to kill you. He must know he's not gonna get away with that."

If I was him, I'd be shaking in my shoes, not packing up to come to Brutham. Although, I

167

wouldn't be him, because when I tried to kill people, I succeeded. That was one of the reasons I preferred the direct approach. Bombs and gases, they're too hit and miss. A good gunshot to the brain, or sliced throat, were much simpler and more effective. Not to mention much more personal.

Waiting to hear through the grapevine whether or not your victim died, would be very unsatisfying. That was a level of patience I didn't have.

"If he wants to be considered for the head of the family, he has no choice but to come here," Lila said. "It might be that he didn't necessarily intend to kill us. That was his way of throwing his hat into the ring, of letting us know he's in contention too."

"Nothing says 'I'm not necessarily trying to kill you' like a bomb," Chloe said dryly.

"It wasn't a very powerful bomb," Lila pointed out. Her brow was furrowed, contradicting her own words with an expression that clearly said she was remembering the explosion. She tried to let on that she wasn't bothered by it, but I knew her better than that.

I sat forward. "Enough to kill you if you were too close to it." For a while there, I thought we'd lost her. For the second time in only a handful of days, I was worried. Seeing her alive and whole…

Words couldn't express my relief. And my anger.

"But I wasn't." She gave me a soft look. One that melted me in places I hadn't known existed before I met her. I would have said I was made of stone and cum. I refused to be soft, but for her I'd be slightly less rigid.

"So we're supposed to let him transfer here and welcome him with open arms?" I asked, borderline disbelieving.

"Exactly," Lila said. "You've made no secret you want to build a bridge between the Bell and Brantley families. Let Zachary think you were using me to achieve that, but now he's put his hand up, you'd rather work with him. Tell him you think men deserve to be in charge. Whatever you have to do. When you've won him over, then we can strike."

"We're going to have to be very convincing for him to believe we're on his side." Parker looked doubtful.

"If anyone can bullshit, it's you two," Dane said. "You've had lots of experience. I, for one, would totally buy the suggestion you're only using Lila to get what you want." He gave Parker a scathing look.

Chloe put a hand on his knee.

"You can be next in line to have your balls ripped off and shoved down your throat, if you like," I said darkly. "In fact, I don't mind if you're first in line."

Dane rolled his eyes. "Typical Brantley. You

throw out the threats, but we all know you're not going to follow through. Your brains are as big as your dicks."

"Thank you," I replied. "Both are very big. It's nice of you to acknowledge that." I gave him a nod, coupled with a sarcastic smile.

Dane barked a laugh. He opened his mouth to say something else, no doubt something derogatory.

"That's enough," Lila snapped. "I know we've been at each other's throats all year, but we need to put that aside. This may come as a shock to some of you, but we're all adults here. It's time we started acting like it. If we don't, we'll be dead at the end of this. If you want to keep carrying on like this, you can fuck off right now, because I'm not going to let childish behaviour get me killed." Her gaze swept across all of us.

I turned to Parker. "That was hot."

"It really was." He nodded. He raised his hands to either side. "I can be a mature adult. If the rest of them can."

"I can," I said. "Lila is right. Fighting amongst ourselves is going to work in Zachary's favour. Him and anyone here who is working for or with him. That's another thing. We can't assume he's going to act alone. It would be naive to presume it's six against one. He's not stupid enough to come here with odds like that. Especially not while Lila and Chloe are alive."

"Good point," Slade said. "There were a couple of new transfers in the last month or so, but no one that stood out. No one else with the last name Sinclair, or anything that ties them to his mother or Samuel Bell."

"It's more likely whoever they are, they already attend Brutham," Dane reasoned.

"Or work here." Parker raised an eyebrow in Dane's direction.

"Or work here," Dane agreed. "But I'm not one of them. My loyalty is with Chloe. To the point where I've put myself off side with the rest of my family." He didn't look too worried about that. Of course not. He was more ambitious than he was sentimental.

"Asher wouldn't care," I said. "No one has seen Mina for years." That was the official story anyway. I'd find myself smothered by a pillow in the middle of the night, courtesy of Reuben, if I deviated from that.

"That leaves Rose. I can see why you'd be worried." Rose DiMarco was intelligent, tough and connected. If anyone wanted to cover their tracks, they went to her. If she couldn't deal with it, no one could. If she was pissed off enough at Dane, she could make him disappear without a trace, and never break a sweat.

Dane shrugged. "I can handle Rose. The point is, I'm not working with Zachary Sinclair." He turned his head to look at Slade.

"Don't look at me," Slade said. "I've never met the guy. He's lucky he's not studying business law, because I won't be teaching him. From what I've seen, he's studying chemistry."

"With a little bit of bomb making on the side," I added. "Useful skills to have, unless he's the enemy. In which case, not so much."

"Lucky for us, we have three computer nerds in our corner," Parker said. "Me, Hunter and Kennedy. Between us, there's nothing we can't hack."

"There's nothing *Kennedy* can't hack," Chloe said. "Maybe she can make a virus like she did with Dad's computer."

"Can't hurt to ask." I shrugged.

"Unless her boyfriends get pissed off at us for asking," Parker remarked. "Then we can look forward to a couple of weeks chained to the ceiling and tortured by Ice Miller. Actually, from what I've heard of him, we wouldn't need to piss them off. He'd just do it for fun."

"He probably has a grudge against you two for turning Kennedy and him in to Dad," Lila said.

Parker grinned. "Nothing we can't handle. All of that turned out fine in the end."

"I doubt Ice sees it that way." She rubbed her eyes. She looked tired. Almost dying would do that to a person. So would almost dying twice. "I suspect he'd happily chain me up beside you two."

"If he tries, his life expectancy will be very short," Slade growled.

"Fuck yeah it will," I agreed. "Better if Lila stays away from Dusk Bay altogether. At least from Ice, Mannix and Ares. All three of them seem like the type to hold a grudge."

Me, I didn't bother, unless it was someone like Zachary. Even Chloe was all right when she wasn't trying to make life difficult for Lila. Dane wasn't so bad either, more or less. And it was easy to get a rise out of him. That was a bonus.

Of course, the minute Lila called an end to their ceasefire, all bets would be off again. We'd be right back to finding ways to make their lives hell, or shortening them.

"Let's see what this Zachary asshole has to say for himself when he gets here," I concluded. "Parker and I will do whatever we have to do, then we'll hit him hard. The prick won't see us coming."

"Dane and I will keep an eye out for any students we suspect might be acting with Zachary," Slade said. "In the meantime, it's probably a good idea for Lila and Chloe to pretend they're still at war with each other. If he sees they've joined forces, is much more likely to suspect they will come after him."

"Right," Dane agreed. "From what I know about this guy he's not stupid. He's probably desperate. We can use that against him."

I rubbed my hands together. I wasn't sure if killing Zachary immediately wasn't the right way to go, but if this was how Lila wanted to play it, then I might as well have some fun.

When we were done with him, Zachary would be lucky to recognise himself in the mirror. If he looked in it. Even his reflection was going to hate him when we were done with him.

CHAPTER 18

HUNTER

"Hey." I flopped down on the grass beside Zachary. Parker on the other side of him. "Welcome to Brutal Academy."

Zachary didn't turn his eyes away from the rugby match until the big forward smashed the hooker into the ground in a bruising tackle. Only when they were staggering to their feet did he turn to look at me.

"Brantley," he said by way of greeting.

I held out my hand. "Hunter. That's Parker." My hand still out, I gestured to my twin.

Zachary looked at my hand for a while before shaking it. "Zachary Sinclair. But you knew that already."

"Yeah, I did." I crossed my legs at my ankles and leaned back on one hand. I turned my gaze to the rugby as the referee called a knock-on and stopped the play for a few moments.

"You like a bit of football? The Brutham Bears aren't bad."

"I like anything where blood is spilled," Zachary said. "As long as it's not mine." He glanced over at me again.

I chuckled. "Man after my own heart. I much prefer other people's blood be spilled than mine."

"Me too," Parker remarked. His eyes were on the game, but he was listening to us.

"So… You grew up with Chloe and Lila Bell." I might as well cut to the chase. We all knew this wasn't a social call.

"Yeah, and you're dating Lila. Both of you." Zachary smiled as the big forward tackled another player. When the man rose, he had blood pouring out of his nose and down his face.

Zachary looked as though the sight made him want to pull out his cock and get himself off.

I couldn't judge. I was turned on by worse things.

"I wouldn't say we're dating her," I said lightly. "We're both fucking her. So have you."

The thought of it made me want to tackle him to the ground and punch the crap out of him. Even though that happened before we met Lila, the idea of him touching her…

Parker snorted. "Who hasn't? She's not exactly a blushing virgin."

Zachary relaxed slightly. He was a long way from trusting us, but he was almost sure we hadn't come to kill him. Not today.

"She was before I got to her," he said with a shrug. "After I fucked Chloe, Lila practically begged me to fuck her. She couldn't stand her sister having something she didn't. Of course, I was happy to oblige. If there's something she's good at, it's spreading her legs."

I laughed as naturally as I could. For talking about her like that, I wanted to slowly slice his dick off.

Instead, I said, "She really is. Her and Chloe must have fucked half the school by now. On the other hand, so have Parker and I. Out here in the sticks, there's nothing much else to do when we're not studying. We might as well stick our cocks into anything that stays still long enough. Right, Park?"

"Yep." Parker grinned.

"So, I was thinking," I said after we watched a couple more minutes of the game. No more blood was spilled, but one of the guys left the field with a head injury that would probably result in a nasty concussion. No one ever said rugby was a pleasant game. It was a brutal blood sport that spoke to the primal part of me. One I preferred to watch than play.

Cricket and tennis were more my speed. Less chance of getting myself badly injured.

"Don't hurt yourself," Zachary teased lightly.

Parker and I both laughed, him a little louder than me.

I clapped Zachary on the back. I would have preferred to knife him there. For Lila's sake, I'd keep playing this stupid game. It would be Zachary who won the stupid prizes.

"Seriously though. Park and I both appreciate the way you went after Chloe and Lila. Teddy bears?" I mimed a chef's kiss. "Genius. I'm definitely stealing that idea and putting it in my playbook. But I want to know why."

Zachary stiffened. "Why what?" He was very much on alert now.

"Why go after them in a way that they didn't end up dead? Was it your intention to kill them or are you sending a message?" I looked hopeful.

He chose his words carefully. "If I wanted to kill them, they'd be dead."

I doubted that, but I played along. "So, you were trying to tell them something? Or were you trying to…encourage them to step aside? I mean, you're older than them and you're a guy. It seems to me you're the easy pick to take Samuel Bell's place some day. They needed a reminder of that. Right?"

I could see the wheels of thought turning in his brain. He wanted to agree with everything I said, but could he trust me? If I was him, I'd tell me to fuck off. But then again, I knew me better than he did.

Finally, he let out a frustrated sigh. "He should have chosen me instead of pitting the girls against each other. Neither of them have the balls to take Sam's place."

"Exactly," I agreed. Lila had bigger proverbial balls than he would ever have. Although, he was smart enough and ruthless enough to have been an asset if he hadn't gone after them. Whatever, that was his funeral.

"They don't have balls at all, which is half the problem." I uncrossed my legs and crossed them the other way. "Sooner or later, they'll get pregnant and get all weak and weepy. You know what women are like. That's why men rule the world."

I caught a glimpse of Parker's smirk at my words. He didn't buy them any more than I did, but only Zachary had to.

"They should both step aside before they break a nail," Parker said. "It's bad enough when that happens."

"What are you saying?" Zachary asked. "I was under the impression you supported Lila."

I gestured vaguely. "Like I said, we're fucking her. For a while we thought maybe she'd be the one to back. Over Chloe anyway. That was before there was a viable alternative." I clapped him on the back again.

"What's in it for you?" He narrowed his eyes at me.

"Power," Parker said.

I nodded my agreement. "The possibility of joining the Bell and Brantley families together. Reuben will never agree to work with a woman. But someone like you— You could change all of that. Imagine how powerful the three of us could be."

"Do you mean how powerful Reuben and I would be?" Zachary asked. "He is the head of your family."

"That's what we want him to think," Parker said. "But Hunt and I have been building contacts over the years. At some point we may move to take Reuben down and replace him. For now, he's useful to us."

If Reuben heard any of that, he'd have someone slice the skin of our bodies as slowly as possible. He was already suspicious that we might not toe the line forever. Anything that sounded like an active plan to overthrow him would get us dead quickly.

The truth was, we had no such plan. Parker and I took every day as it came. Besides, we had several other brothers we'd have to step over first and taking all of them on would take time and resources.

Resources we'd have when Lila was head of her family.

"You'd support me against Chloe and Lila?" Zachary asked carefully.

"Absolutely we would," I agreed. "In fact, I'd like to nominate you to join the Brotherhood."

"The Brotherhood?" Zachary echoed.

"It's a very exclusive club of the most powerful men in the world," I said. "There's a chapter here at Brutham. Most of us join here, but only when invited and nominated by a current member. Once you join, you're in for life. The Brotherhood of Kings has connections you could only dream of."

"I've never heard of it." Zachary shook his head.

Parker laughed. "It wouldn't be a very good secret organisation if you had. Trust me, you know the names of a lot of the members. They're basically the who's who of the most rich and powerful, and the up-and-comers in the world. But don't ask us to tell you who, because you don't get to know unless you join."

"Both of you are members?" He still looked doubtful.

"We are," I said. "We were nominated by our brother Joshua. Most of our brothers are members."

The only one who wasn't was Zeke. He had no interest in any of that. Sometimes I wondered if he was adopted. He was certainly not as much fun as the rest of us.

"What do I have to do to join?" Zachary asked.

"There's a meeting two nights from now," I said. "If you want to go, the committee will interview you and if you pass that, you'll go through initiation. Don't worry, it's nothing you can't handle."

Zachary nodded. "I'm there."

Of course he was. No one could resist the lure of a secret, powerful organisation. I certainly couldn't. Like him, I'd had no idea it existed before I started at Brutham. If every member was in the same place and we were attacked and killed, the world would fall into chaos. We were exactly that influential. Nothing happened in the world that didn't involve one of us in some way.

"Excellent." I grinned. "I don't know about you two, but I'm thirsty. Let's go to the bar and celebrate our new arrangement." I could use a beer or three to wash the taste of bullshit out of my mouth.

I climbed to my feet. Before I could take more than a step or two, Zachary put a hand on my bicep.

"There are no women in this... Brotherhood are there?"

I laughed. "Of course not. Unless you count the

Fillies. Women who connect themselves to members of the Brotherhood. Some work at the Brotherhood's clubs in the hope of catching the eye of one. We usually pass them around until either someone marries them or we get tired of them."

They were usually gorgeous and ambitious. If the Brotherhood allowed women, they'd be the first to join. Instead, they stayed on the fringes, pouring drinks and spreading their legs. Most of them benefited by receiving gifts, or marrying a rich husband.

Lila would throw herself off the roof of the Academy before she became a Filly. If they ever changed their policy, I'd nominate her in a heartbeat, but the Brotherhood had operated the same way for at least two hundred years. It wasn't going to change now. Not unless Parker and I could work our way into the ruling committee. Then we may have a chance. That would take decades. No one was going to listen to a pair of twenty-year old university students.

Zachary smiled. I could almost see him hungering for women willing to fuck him for his power. If he wasn't careful, that shit would go to his head.

"So, about that drink," I said.

"Let's go," Zachary said. "You two aren't what I expected, but we definitely have something to celebrate here. The beginning of something immense."

"It couldn't get bigger than you heading the Bell family," Parker agreed. He rubbed his hands together. "This is going to be so much fun. And hey, we can talk about helping you through the trials. We know all the good spots to dispose of your enemies. If they're still standing by then."

"By the time the trials come, Chloe and Lila will both be on their knees," Zachary said. "Where they belong."

"Choking on our cocks." I grinned.

CHAPTER 19

HUNTER

I groaned. My head pounded. My whole body felt heavy, like it was weighted down. I must have lain in the same position for too long.

I tried to roll over, but I couldn't move. Had I really drunk that much? I couldn't remember beyond my second beer.

Zachary had peppered Parker and I with questions about the Brotherhood, and ways we could help him with the trials. I'd been as evasive as I could without looking like I was avoiding the questions, and stuck to small talk, like what courses he was taking and whether he had any ambitions outside heading the Bell family.

Everything after that was blank.

I groaned and tried again to roll over. At first, I thought my body felt like lead. In the back of my aching mind I realised something else was going on. It wasn't that my body didn't want to move, but that I *couldn't.*

I opened my crusty eyes a crack and blinked to clear them. The room was dim, but this was not my bedroom at the Academy. Not Lila's either, nor Parker's. It didn't look like anywhere inside the Academy building.

The floor underneath was cold and hard. Concrete. Judging by the faint smell of decay and dirt, I wasn't in Brutham anymore. Unless this was one of the outlying sheds. If it was, it wasn't the one Parker and I usually used.

"Hunt?" Parker's voice sounded dry and raw.

I swallowed and found my throat to be the same. It tasted of something nasty. Not beer or even vomit, but something sickly sweet and medicinal.

"I'm right here, Park," I whispered. God, I could use a drink of water around about now. If my headache didn't kill me, my thirst would.

I tried to raise my arms, but they were heavy as fuck. Chained, with metal bound firmly around my wrists.

I was into being tied up as much as the next guy, but not like this. My strong preference was for consent.

"Where is here?" Parker asked. "What the fuck happened? My head is killing me."

"Mine too and I don't know," I said. "Shhh."

"What—"

I hissed at him to be quiet. Footsteps approached, accompanied by voices.

"I'm sorry I doubted you." That was Zachary. "I didn't think they'd fall for any of that, but they all did exactly what you said they'd do."

"Of course they did."

My whole body stiffened more than it already was. That was Chloe. She sounded as smug as hell.

"Everything went almost exactly as we planned," she continued. "It might have been easier if Lila died from the shit in that teddy bear you gave her, but this worked out better, don't you think?"

"Yeah, it did; Lila still thinks you're working with her." Zachary sounded amused. "And we got these two assholes out of the way."

Who was this prick calling an asshole? As soon as I got out of here, he was going to hell, because I was going to send him there. After torturing him for a while.

"Which one can I kill first?" Zachary sounded excited for the possibility.

"Neither one for now," Chloe said. "While they're alive, we can use them as leverage. Once they've outdone their usefulness, I'll decide. Or better yet, we could get them to kill each other."

Zachary laughed. "That would be good for shits and giggles."

I was going to send both of them to hell. As slowly and painfully as possible. I'd start by cutting off their toes, and gradually work my way up, avoiding vital organs and too much bleeding as I went. Just for fun, I might even carve my initials into their foreheads. And then, into their bones. If Parker was lucky, I'd let him join in too.

Parker grunted softly in annoyance. Only loud enough for me to hear. He obviously realised it was better they didn't know we were awake and listening.

"And Lila?" Zachary asked. "Are you going to kill her too?"

He was obviously very much her minion, just like Lila suspected he was. They must have planted that second teddy bear and timed it to look like Zachary went after Chloe.

That was fucked up bullshit. Chloe wanted Lila to trust her and she had; enough to let her guard down. Enough to send us to make friends with Zachary. If the taste in my mouth was any indication, he'd spiked our drinks with something nasty but nonlethal.

No, I'd watched him carefully, keeping my drink to myself. Parker had bought the first round and I'd bought the second. Zachary hadn't gone near my drink. It was the asshole behind the bar, working with Zachary and Chloe.

He was going to hell with them.

"I don't see any reason we can't continue with our original plan," Chloe said. "Things will be so much easier with Dad if she tells him she's dropping out of the running. He'll accept her quitting better than he'll accept me killing her. He always had a soft spot for her." She sounded bitter.

"He thinks she's as ruthless as he is, and you're not," Zachary said. "But she doesn't know you as well as I do." A slight slap of skin hitting the wall was followed by the wet sound of them kissing.

Did Dane know Chloe and Zachary were involved? More than involved, if their already rapid breathing was an indication.

A zipper slid undone, fabric rustled. She sighed low, from the back of her throat.

"Fuck, you always feel so good," Zachary moaned. "So. Fucking. Good." He was obviously thrusting with each word.

How long had they been fucking each other? I guessed it was a while.

"I'm so glad you transferred here." Chloe's voice

was breathless. "I missed you."

"You missed my cock," he growled. "You missed being my whore. Didn't you? *Didn't you?*"

"Yes," she moaned. "Yes, I missed being your whore. Mmmm, I'm going to… To come."

"Good, come for me, bitch," Zachary told her.

Evidently she liked dirty talk from him as just much as she liked it from Dane. She cried out Zachary's name, moaning loudly as she came.

If my head didn't hurt enough before, it was worse now, listening to them fucking. For once, I wasn't even slightly turned on. If anything, my cock was softer than it had ever been in my life. No doubt that was the side effect of whatever drug was still in my system. It better wear off, or they'd be lucky to go to hell.

The sound of skin hitting the wall came faster, over and over, accompanied by Zachary's grunts and groans and growls.

"I'm going to come inside you, you dirty slut." He growled one more time before he came.

Was ear bleach a thing? Because I was going to need a butt ton of it after this.

I thought listening to Chloe and Dane was trau-matising, but it was nothing to this. Neither of them had tried to kill Lila at the time. Now, I was tied here, listening to my enemies make each other feel good.

Ugh, kill me now.

What did Parker and I do to deserve this? Okay, we did a lot of shitty things and killed people, but this was a cruel and unusual torture. Mercifully it was over quickly. Apparently Zachary didn't have much staying power. Certainly not as much as Dane.

They were silent for a while, catching their breath.

"Are we leaving them here?" Zachary asked finally. "We're too close to the Academy for my liking."

"For now," Chloe said easily. "No one will find them here. No one will think to look." She sounded certain of that.

Did she really think we could just disappear off the face of the planet and no one would notice? If she did, she was delusional.

"Dane said no one ever comes here," she added.

"He better be right," Zachary growled. "What about his involvement in all of this anyway? He's a DiMarco."

It sounded like there was trouble in paradise. Maybe Zachary-boy didn't like to share his stepsister with a teacher.

"He's useful," Chloe said. "Just like you are. He's in this with us until the end."

"I have to keep sharing?" Zachary sounded pissed off.

"You knew going into this there would be other men," she scolded. "I'm with you and I'm with Dane. And I'm with anyone else who is useful to me. I will fuck whomever I have to fuck, whenever I have to fuck them. And if I tell you to fuck someone—"

"I won't cheat on you," he argued.

"It's not cheating if I tell you to do it," she said. "You know what's at stake here. More power than you and I could ever dream of. We need to do whatever it takes." Her tone turned sultry. "Would you do that for me?"

"I'll do anything for you." He sounded sulky. It seemed he had the impression she'd drop everyone for him. "You're not going to ask me to screw Lila, are you?"

I curled my hands into fists. If that prick touched a hair on her head I would personally place his feet into acid, then pour some of that onto his cock and balls. Better yet, I'd cover them with honey and tie him on top of an ant's nest. The ways I'd make him suffer would be worse than anything his worst nightmares could conjure.

"I doubt she'd trust you, but it wouldn't hurt to try." Chloe said. "With the twins away, she may need consoling."

"But Slade—"

"We need to deal with him," she said with a sigh.

"Dane is keeping an eye on him for now, but we definitely shouldn't underestimate Mr Lincoln. I wish I'd got his attention before she did. I might work on him, he might come over to our side yet."

"If you fuck him…"

"It will be because it's necessary," she said firmly. "Besides, he's kinda hot. I can understand what Lila sees in him."

Zachary made a rude noise. That was followed by the sound of skin hitting skin like she was patting his cheek.

"You'll forget your jealousy when you have more pussy than you know what to do with."

"I only want yours." He sounded frustrated.

"You say that now, but that will change. You'll have them lining up to wrap their lips around your cock."

"Speaking of that," he said slowly. "They wanted to nominate me for something called the Brotherhood."

His words were followed by her sharp intake of breath.

"So it's a real thing?" he asked.

"It is. I didn't expect them to suggest that to you," she replied. "It's not something that's offered around to someone you barely know. Did they seem sincere?"

"I guess so," he said uncertainly. "Probably not

now. Should I have abandoned the plan to bring them here?"

Silence was followed by, "I don't think so. You can always ask Dad to nominate you. Unless he's used all his nominations. Each member is allowed six in their lifetime."

"They really don't allow women?" he asked carefully. He sounded like he didn't want to admit he liked the idea of women being passed around the organisation. He wasn't sure what she'd think if she knew.

"They really don't, but beyond that I don't know much about it," she admitted. "If anyone offers to nominate you again, say yes. Getting you in there could really help us."

"Yeah, if they do. Anyway, we should get to class."

"Yes we should, I'll be back later to check on our guests." She laughed softly.

I can't fucking wait, I thought.

Their voices and footsteps faded before a door opened and closed somewhere a few metres away.

"Well this is fucked up," Parker said.

"That's one way to put it," I agreed. I swallowed and winced at my dry throat. "We need to find a way to get the hell out of here. Whatever that bitch has planned, I don't think either of us are going to like it."

CHAPTER 20

LILA

"Is everything all right?" Chloe flopped down beside me as I clicked out of my messages and threw my phone down on the table.

"Yeah." I pretended to be interested in my laptop screen, but I hadn't read a word of anything on it for the last hour.

"Just a message from Parker to let me know Reuben needed him and Hunter to do some urgent business." It wasn't unusual, but the timing sucked. Although, the timing always sucked. Reuben seemed to have a knack for knowing when the worst times were, and sending the guys off somewhere.

"It must get really tiring," Chloe said.

When she didn't elaborate, I decided to take the bait anyway.

"What must get tiring?"

"The guys always prioritising their brothers over you." She pulled her phone out of her pocket and toyed with it for a while. "Any time Reuben tells them to jump, they jump without thinking. Have they ever told him no? After what happened to us, there's no way Dane would leave me here alone."

Her words hit too close to home. As far as I know, they never told Reuben they wouldn't do whatever he asked them to. They enjoyed working for him. But to leave now, when so much was at stake?

When I was head of my family, I'd have to consider my options where Reuben was concerned. There may be a time when assassinating him was my only option. He may prove impossible to work with, especially if he was going to keep pulling the strings with the twins. I didn't care for it in the short term, but in the long-term it was definitely not going to work.

"Slade is still here," I reminded her. "And you."

She flashed a brief smile. "Of course I am."

There was definitely something off about her expression. I put it down to this uneasy alliance. *Temporary* alliance. As soon as we dealt with Zachary, we'd be back at war. For all I knew, she was planning her next move.

"Have you spoken to Zachary?" I asked.

She looked even cagier, but shrugged. "I have. He

196

claimed to know nothing about any explosive devices in either of the teddy bears. He actually suggested he was set up by Reuben Brantley. What better way to get rid of us, while pinning it on someone else?"

I mulled that over for a minute. "Is there any chance that's what happened? Maybe Zachary is innocent in all of this."

I *wanted* to believe he wouldn't do anything to hurt me. He'd seemed so sincere when we last spoke. Setting up others wasn't necessarily Reuben's style though. He usually didn't care who knew he was behind attacks like this. Perhaps he saw an opportunity and took it.

"At this point, anything is possible," Chloe agreed. "Maybe we should cut Zachary some slack. Have you talked to him?"

I shook my head. "Not since that night. I saw him arrive, but that was all."

"Maybe you should talk to him," Chloe suggested. She glanced around. "In the meantime, we're still supposed to be on opposite sides. We wouldn't want anyone to see us talking and think we're friendly toward each other."

"Definitely wouldn't want that," I said with an edge of sarcasm. "I guess I could speak to him. I just wish the guys told me what he said to them before they left. I tried calling them, but it went straight to voicemail. I'm sure they'll call me back as soon as they're able to."

They fucking better. Taking off without a word was bad enough, but leaving me in the dark where Zachary was concerned, was worse.

"I'm sure they will." Chloe stood and shoved her phone into the pocket of her skirt. "No doubt, wherever they are, they're pining for you." The smile she gave me before she walked away gave me chills for some reason.

"They better be," I said under my breath. I closed my laptop with a sigh and gathered it up. If I couldn't concentrate in the quiet of the library, then I had no chance. I slipped it under my arm and headed out the oak trimmed doors and up the stairs at the end of the corridor.

Brutham had elevators, but I preferred the stairs. They were good exercise and not an enclosed space like an elevator car. I couldn't step foot in one without being terrified they'd break down and I'd get stuck in there. In my nightmares, the lights would go out and I would hear no sound except my thoughts.

I'd probably never know if my fear of enclosed spaces was due to being locked in the sensory deprivation room in my father's basement as a child, or if it was a phobia I was born with. Either way, I avoided them as much as possible.

I trotted up the steps and around the corner to Slade's office. The door was ajar. I tapped on it before pushing it open.

He glanced up from his computer and gave me a smile that made my heart flip. He was so fucking gorgeous I could hardly believe he looked twice at me, much less tangled his life with mine so quickly.

"I was just thinking about you," he said.

I grimaced playfully and set my things down on a table to the side of the room. "Don't tell me, you're marking my essay?" I closed the door and twisted the lock until it clicked.

"If I said I was, what would you do for a higher grade?" He leaned back in his chair and laced his fingers behind his head.

I stepped over toward him, moving slowly and deliberately. I walked around his desk and knelt down beside him. I ran my hand from his knee, up his thigh and over his cock.

I glanced up at him before working the button of his pants loose and sliding down the zip. He lifted his hips to allow me to ease his pants down to expose his already half hard cock.

I gripped his length in one hand and stroked my

fingers down to his tip and back up to his balls until he was rock hard.

I looked back up at him and watched his expression as I licked his tip like it was a tasty lollipop. I slid my tongue over the bead of pre-cum that formed on the head. He was deliciously salty.

My eyes still on his face, I wrapped my mouth around his cock and took him in as deep as I could. Deep enough for him to tap the back of my throat.

I watched him watching me suck him, getting more and more aroused by his clear enjoyment. I loved nothing more than giving pleasure to the guys I cared about. Controlling their pleasure turned me on harder than anything.

His hips rose and fell off the seat of the chair, as he fucked my mouth in rhythm with my sucks.

"Fuck, that's good," he groaned. "I'm going to come in your mouth."

I smiled around my mouthful and sucked harder, his cock hitting the back of my throat with every thrust. Forget lollipops, cock was better than any of them. So thick, warm and hard.

He grunted in bliss and ground against me as he came, squirting warm, salty cum into my throat so hard I gagged.

I went on sucking until he sagged. Slowly, I slid

my mouth off him and smiled as I swallowed down every drop like it was melted chocolate.

"Does that give me an A?" I asked teasingly.

"I think I can give you a B+. If you want an A, you're going to have to sit on my desk."

Whether or not I wanted an A, I definitely wanted an O. I scrambled to my feet and onto the top of the desk in front of him.

He gripped my knees and drew them apart, making my skirt ride up my thighs.

He held my thighs open, leaned in and exhaled deeply. "Your pussy always smells like perfection."

He pulled the gusset of my G-string aside and ran the pads of two fingers around my pussy and over my clit. He looked like he was admiring one of the wonders of the world.

He slid his fingers down to my entrance and worked his fingertips inside. "So wet for me too." He pressed his fingers in deeper.

He'd slid them all the way to his knuckles when his phone rang. Rather than ignoring it, he picked it up and pressed it to his ear. At the same time, he slid his fingers in and out of me. The heel of his hand brushed my clit.

"Hello?" he said into the phone. He listened while he worked me with his skilled fingers. His brow crinkled in a frown and his nose scrunched slightly, adorably.

He glanced at me and mouthed, "Shhh."

I bit my lip to keep from moaning when he hooked his fingers around, massaging me inside and out while whoever was on the other end of the phone spoke.

"I see," he was saying. "That could be a problem."

I leaned back on my hands, hooked my fingers around the edge of the desk while my back arched. I bucked my hips and bit my lip harder to stop myself from screaming at the ceiling. Fuck, his touch was so good.

"Yes. No, I agree. It's nothing we can't deal with." He glanced up at me, a wicked glint in his eyes. He knew I was close and fully intended to stay on the line while I came.

I ground against his hand as he pushed me closer and closer to the edge.

A groan slipped from between my lips.

He glanced at me sharply. "No, don't worry about it. Trust me, I have the situation well in hand." He grinned.

I made a face at him, but went on rocking until I tipped over the edge of the abyss and into a rolling tide of pleasure. I came so hard around his hand I left his fingers drenched. I dug my nails into the wood to hold back my cry.

My heart raced as I drifted back down to earth.

"All right, I'll talk to you later," he told whoever was on the other end of the phone. "Okay, bye." He ended the call and placed his phone down on the desk.

"Well, that was fun." He slid his fingers out of my pussy and pressed them between my lips. "Suck."

I sucked, tasting myself on his skin.

"You're fascinating," he told me. "You like to be in control, but you know how to relinquish it and do what you're told. You could have screamed the building down while I was on that important call. But you didn't. You were nice and quiet, just like I told you. Except that one groan." He looked stern.

"Sorry, sir," I said sweetly. "I couldn't contain myself with you touching me like that. Does that mean I don't get an A?" I pouted playfully.

I knew for a fact I wouldn't earn my marks on my back. If my work sucked, no amount of blowjobs would convince him to give me a higher grade. I would have hated that anyway. I worked hard to do well with my brain, not my mouth. Not my pussy either. Not to mention the fact Brutham wouldn't turn a blind eye to our relationship if he did that.

"You already got an A," he growled. 'Your essay

was beautifully done, but for that groan, you've earned yourself punishment."

I smiled. "Are you going to give me detention?"

"Detention is for high school," he replied. "What I have in mind will be a lot more fun."

He took my hands and pulled me forward until I hopped off his desk. "Come with me."

"Yes, sir." I followed him out of his office.

CHAPTER 21

LILA

Zachary looked up in alarm as I stopped in front of him. His beer was halfway to his mouth. He hesitated, then lowered it.

"Hey," he said warily. "May I remind you there's a lot of people in the bar right now. Lots of witnesses if you try to kill me."

"Funny," I slid onto the couch beside him. I tried to suppress a wince at the lingering pain in my ass cheeks. Slade wasn't kidding when he said he was going to punish me. I loved every moment of it. I even loved the bruises he left on my thighs and wrists and the bite marks on my breasts and throat. The man was feral, in the best way possible.

"I was going to say the same to you." I crossed my legs, not missing the way his gaze slid up my jeans-covered legs and over my chest. He always looked at me like I was a tasty snack.

"Why would I want to kill you?" he asked. "You're my sister." He shrugged but he hadn't lost the wary expression.

"You tell me," I said smoothly. "Where did you get that teddy bear?"

He sighed. "Is that what this is about? I swear, I had no idea there was anything dangerous inside… What was his name? Herman."

He looked desperate for me to believe him. "I bought both bears online from what looked like a reputable website. Not one on the dark web that sells booby-trapped plush toys. If they even exist. I had no way of knowing someone set the website up for me to find it, or changed the bears out, or whatever. All I wanted was to do something nice for my sisters."

He raised a hand as though he might put it on my knee, but then lowered it back to his own leg.

Wise move, given Slade was only a few metres away, watching surreptitiously. I couldn't guarantee what he might do if Zachary touched me. I doubted it would end well for my former stepbrother.

"Do you want to take over the family from Dad?" I asked bluntly.

He licked his lips. Picked up his beer and took a gulp.

"Honestly… If he offered it to me, I'd accept. But he's not going to offer it to me. The best I can hope for is that you don't blame me for what happened with the bear, and keep an open mind about letting me work for you. I can prove my loyalty. I can prove that my tongue is still as skilled as ever."

He forced a smile. For the first time in years, he gave me the impression fucking me was something he was reluctant to do.

I put it down to his not wanting to share me with the twins, and Slade. Maybe he met someone here at Brutham already. That wouldn't surprise me. No one here wasted time snapping anyone who would be an asset to them, now or in the future.

Either way, it didn't matter. I wasn't going to go there with him.

"You can keep your tongue to yourself," I told him. "I have enough of those to keep me busy." I took the beer from his hand, gave him a cheeky smile and sipped.

"You really had no idea Herman was full of deadly fumes? What about the bear you gave to Chloe? The one that exploded after I threw it out the window. I had a feeling someone was watching, waiting for the right time."

He shrugged and crossed his arms, relinquishing ownership of his drink. "Would you be so surprised if Reuben Brantley had a camera in your sister's bedroom?" He scoffed. "Hell, I wouldn't be surprised if Hunter and Parker put it there. Maybe you should be having this conversation with them."

"I will when they get back from their business trip." I hated to admit that he might be right, but if there was a camera in Chloe's room, chances were the twins put it there. Not so they could blow me up. They might have done it at Reuben's request, or so they could keep an eye on Chloe.

Zachary was watching me closely. "Are you sure you can trust them? They seem ambitious and very, very… Brantley. Betrayal is in their blood. I wouldn't put it past either of them to get a kick out of using you until they're done with you."

Before I could respond to that he added, "Or you might be using them to get some dick while you keep an eye on them. You know what they say about keeping your enemies close."

"Of course I can trust them," I argued.

I didn't want to admit he planted the seeds of doubt in the back of my mind. I'd always known I needed to be careful of Hunter and Parker. They weren't referred to as the evil twins for nothing. Their whole family was known for stepping on other people to get what they wanted. I wasn't naïve enough to think they might do the same to me.

I didn't want to believe that though. My feelings for both of them ran deep. The idea they might be planning to betray me, made my heart twist. If they did, it would be the last thing they ever did.

"I know you better than that," Zachary said softly. "The Lila Bell I know doesn't go around trusting people easily. You're always on alert for anyone putting a toe out of line. Nothing gets past you, because you don't take things at face value. You're always thinking, evaluating and planning. Just like your father."

It wasn't an accusation, just an observation. An accurate one, most of the time.

"You're right, I don't trust people easily. Including you," I told him.

I wasn't sure I believed a word of what he said about the teddy bears. The best lies always have enough truth in them to make them plausible. Would I have been like this if I grew up with my mother?

I felt as though I spent my life surrounded by men and shadows, and a sister who always seemed to be looking for ways to take advantage.

"Including me," he agreed. "And Chloe. You need to consider the possibility she did this. She might have been planning something with the other teddy bear, that you ruined by turning up when you did. She said something about you cutting it open and finding the bomb inside. Maybe doing that set it off? Explosives are fragile. If you do the wrong thing at the wrong time, they can blow up in your face. Literally."

"Maybe you and Chloe are working together," I said lightly.

He stiffened slightly, then snorted. "Maybe. Did hell freeze over?" He leaned over towards me.

"I meant what I said, I want to work with you. In whatever capacity that may be. I'm not asking you to marry me or have my children, just let me be a part of this." He spread his hands and gestured towards me. "I don't think that's too much to ask."

He seemed sincere, but there was something about his tone that set off warning bells in the back of my mind. Nothing I could put my finger on. Just a sense that something was… Off.

"If I do have you work for me," I said slowly, "it won't be in teddy bear acquisitions." Even if there was such a thing, which there probably wasn't. Although, those teddy bears had to come from somewhere.

He laughed. "I promise not to buy any more teddy bears. Or plush elephants. Or plush pigs. Or plush anything."

"Good, because I don't think I could trust a plush anything ever again." I finished the last of his drink and placed the empty glass on the table in front of us.

"That's the Lila Bell I know," he said. "Mistrustful of everything, including plush toys."

"It might not be my preferred lifestyle choice, but it is what it is." I shrugged.

A frown brushed his forehead. "What would be your preferred lifestyle choice? If you could be anything you want. Anything at all, what would you choose? Would you choose the same lifestyle as Sam and the rest of the Bell family? Or would you walk away and do something completely different?"

"I don't get to choose—"

He cut me off. "If you *did* get to choose. If you could walk out the door right now and go and live your best, ideal life, what would you do?"

"I don't know," I said slowly. "Maybe I'd just get a regular job, get married and live in the suburbs." That sounded harmless, but as boring as hell.

He raised his eyebrows at me. "Doubtful. Try again."

I rolled my eyes at him. "Fine. I think I'd start a company and build it from scratch to something huge. Maybe an airline, or a line of boutique clothing stores."

"CEO of an airline," he mused. "Lila Air, to rival Devlin Air."

"Something like that." Devlin Air started as a small company, but under the leadership of Anderson Devlin, the oldest of the six Devlin Brothers, was now a billion-dollar company, with offices all over the world. Apparently Anderson Devlin was a massive asshole, but he was a wealthy one.

"If anyone could do that, it would be you," Zachary said. "Have you ever thought about walking away? You have enough money to start whatever company you want. A legitimate one."

I snorted. "You sound like Chloe. Maybe you should have this conversation with her. That would solve all of our problems." Some of them anyway.

"You could both walk away," he suggested.

"And leave you to take over from Dad?" Was that what he was getting at here?

"Would that be so bad?" he asked. "Look, I'm not saying you should walk away for my benefit, but think about doing it for yours. How long do you think the family can go on defying the law? What if it catches up and you're at the helm? You would be locked away for the rest of your life. Is that what you want?"

I smirked. "Have you forgotten how easy it is to pay to have any number of things disappear? Even if the law caught up, there's nothing they can do. No one I can't pay off. Honestly, any investigator would know that and not bother to come sniffing around anyway. They could spend years trying to pin things on us and we'd just walk away from it. Their time would be better spent investigating matters that can be prosecuted. Or crimes that aren't victimless, like husbands hitting their wives."

There was nothing I hated more than a bully. If anyone in my organisation was violent towards their partner without their consent, they could look forward to being buried alive. I didn't tolerate it.

"I guess so." He didn't look convinced. "I want what's best for you, okay? I'd hate it if you looked back someday and regretted not walking away when you had the chance. Once you're head of the family, it's going to be a lot more difficult to untangle your-self from that web."

"This is what I want," I said firmly. "If Chloe wants to turn her back on the family, she's welcome to do that, but I won't. Hell, if you want to walk away with her, I'll support that. But I've never backed down from a fight and I'm not going to start now."

"Neither am I," he said quickly. "Whatever happens, I'm not backing down either. I'm in this thing until the bitter end." He nodded to punctuate that declaration. "So, you believe me about the teddy bears? That it wasn't me?"

I sighed. "I don't know what to believe. But I will

say this. If I find out it was you, or if you do anything to betray me, I will kill you. With my bare hands if I have to."

He sat back, a guarded expression on his face. "Noted." He looked like he had more to say, but he fell silent after that.

CHAPTER 22

LILA

"The twins?"

I looked up from frowning at my screen to see Slade watching me with concern.

He nodded towards my phone. "You were looking at that like you weren't impressed. Is it the twins? Have they finally checked in?"

It was five days since they went off for whatever Reuben needed them for. Apart from a couple of text messages, I hadn't heard a thing. They'd probably turn up in a couple of days with tans, and act like nothing happened.

"No, it's not them." I put my phone aside and finished my coffee. Like everything else here, the food was amazing. The best coffee money could buy. Of course it was, we did better with a good breakfast every day. Whatever Brutham Academy had to do to maintain a high academic standard, they'd do. The school board ruthlessly hunted down the best chefs and the best ingredients and paid well for them.

Slade raised an eyebrow at me expectantly.

I sighed. "My father is coming. He'll be here in about twenty minutes."

"Let me guess, he likes to spring visits on you at the last minute?" Slade bit down into his toast and washed it down with tea. I'd never seen him drink coffee. As far as I know, he didn't.

"Exactly," I said. "If I knew he was coming, I'd have time to run."

Slade grinned at the expression on my face. "You wouldn't really run."

"No, but some days it's tempting." I looked at him over the rim of my cup and wondered if I dared to ask.

"I'm coming with you," he said before I could ask. "I'm not leaving you to go into the hornet's nest alone. He's your father but I trust him as much as I trust anyone else in your family."

"Only an idiot would turn their back on my father," I said. "I sure as fuck wouldn't. On some level, he loves me, but he's not above using me to get what he wants. You know what they say about blood being thicker than water? The only thing thicker than that is ambition, and my father has plenty of that to spare. If it was in his best interest to burn Chloe and me, he'd do it. He wouldn't even think twice."

"He sounds like my father," Slade said sympathetically. "Mine was always looking for an excuse to use the belt on me. My sisters felt it occasionally too, but mostly it was me."

"He sounds like an asshole," I said. My father punished me, but he never hit me. Although, that might have been better than being locked away in the basement.

"He *was* an asshole." Slade shrugged. "One day I had enough and I wrapped that belt around his neck and pulled until he stopped struggling. None of us shed a tear at his death."

My lips dropped apart. I won't say I haven't been tempted, but I've never seriously considered killing my father. To be that desperate must be horrible.

"How old were you?" I asked softly.

"Twelve." He downed the last of his tea. "I left him lying there on the floor and went off to my first day of high school. The police ruled it a suicide and that was it. They knew what a prick he was, they just couldn't pin anything on him that would stick. I think they were glad to be rid of him too. And I learnt a valuable lesson. That I was capable of standing up for myself and that killing people who deserve it is enjoyable."

"I feel like I shouldn't find that a massive turn on, but I do," I said.

He grinned. "It's part of my charm. So you know, I still have that belt and I'll use it on your father if he gives me a reason."

"I have a feeling that belt has a long history of being around people's necks." I glanced into my coffee cup to find it already empty. I set it aside and rested my elbows on the table.

Slade leaned forward until we were almost nose to nose. "Yes, it does, and you know what? I'd like to put it around your neck while I fuck that pretty little pussy of yours."

That made me all sorts of hot. "How many people have you killed with that belt?"

He looked thoughtful. "Fourteen. It would have been fifteen, but I was only trying to scare the last guy. I almost got carried away."

"Will you get carried away with me?" His breath brushed my cheek, making my heart race.

"Definitely," he agreed. "But not to the point where I squeeze the last breath out of your body. I know exactly how far to go for us both to enjoy it."

"I would much rather do that right now than speak to my father." As it was, I was wet and probably flushed. If that bothered Dad in any way, that was too fucking bad. He could have given me a few hours, or even a few days, warning of his intention to visit. Since he didn't, he got what he got.

"I guess he wouldn't be pleased if we kept him waiting while I fucked your brains out," Slade said with a sigh.

"No one keeps Samuel Bell waiting." I matched his sigh. "He's going to be pissed off enough knowing I'm... Consorting with someone else with Brantley connections."

Which was hypocritical, given Kennedy's boyfriends all worked for the Brantleys.

"Is that what we're doing?" Humour shone in Slade's eyes. "Consorting?"

I snorted softly. "Yeah, that's the fanciest word I can think of for fucking. I was going to go with boinking, but I figured it sounded better."

He laughed. "You might be right. Although, bonking is a very good word. Very descriptive of the way a bed sounds when we're using it right."

I shook my head at him and laughed. "I guess it does. Why do I get the feeling you've given this a lot more thought than I ever have?"

"I'm a guy." He shrugged. "It's my job to make sure your pussy is getting wrecked just right. If I don't, that would be neglectful."

"Would it, now?" I picked up my phone and tucked it into the back pocket of my jeans. "And what happens if you neglect me?"

"I don't know, because I have no intention of doing it," he said. He stacked my plate and cup on his and carried them over to the trolley the staff used to wheel them into the kitchen for washing.

Once we were clear of the dining room, we were free to talk more easily.

"Will your father be seeing Chloe and Zachary too?"

"His message didn't say, but I presume so," I said. "Is not going to come all this way and not at least see Chloe."

"That would be a punch in the guts to Zachary." Slade didn't look particularly sympathetic. He didn't seem to buy what Zachary said about the teddy bears, or much of anything Chloe said.

If I thought I didn't trust easily, I was nothing compared to him. That wasn't too surprising given his childhood. Who would you trust if you were forced to kill your own father at the age of twelve? He was the kind of guy who formed his loyalties and didn't budge.

"My father isn't particularly sentimental." I eyed a couple of students who hurried to get out of my way as I walked down the corridor. They did that everywhere I went. If I didn't put fear into them, my last name would.

"He won't care if he hurts any of our feelings."

"I'm starting to think I should get my belt before we go and meet him," Slade said.

"If we had time, I'd say you should," I said. "He'll be here in two minutes. My father is many things, including punctual." If anything, he was more likely to be early than late.

Slade grabbed my wrist and pulled me to a stop.

"I'm sure my father won't do anything to warrant you getting your belt—" I started to say.

"This isn't about the belt," he said. "This is about you running the family someday. At some point, you need to teach everyone who is in charge. That includes your father."

I frowned. "What are you saying?"

"I'm saying, what's the hurry?" he said lightly. "It won't kill your father to wait for you. What's he going to do about it? Have you killed?"

"No, but he might have you killed if he realises this is your idea." I stepped closer to him and looked up into his eyes. I could happily drown in them. If I wasn't careful, I was going to fall for him and I was going to fall hard. That terrified me almost as much as any dark, silent room. Love made people vulnerable and I couldn't afford to be vulnerable.

On the other hand, sometimes love made people stronger. It was a fine fucking line I didn't dare to cross. Not yet anyway.

"I'd prefer not to give him an excuse," I added. If my father killed Slade, I wouldn't forgive him. What would I do?

How would it feel to wrap Slade's belt around my father's neck and pull it tight? He'd fix his gaze on mine and watch with widening eyes as the air was cut off from his lungs. His body would slump—

I shook my head slightly. He better not give me a reason to act on those thoughts. They were far too compelling.

"I'm not that easy to kill," Slade said easily. "But you know I'm right. If you come running every time he crooks a finger, then he's going to keep doing it. He's going to know he's the boss. Without doubt, he's waiting for you to take the initiative. To stand up to him and show him you're ready to be the boss." He tilted his head slightly, his gaze on my face as his words sank in.

I swallowed hard. The only thing in this world I was afraid of was my father. Specifically what he might do to me if I didn't live up to his high expectations. He wouldn't kill me, but he could do a whole lot worse than that. Worse than choosing Chloe over me. Worse than choosing Zachary over either of us.

If I failed him, he could lock me in the basement and leave me to rot. Or he could... A whirlpool of other horrible things tumbled around in my brain.

Along with that came the realisation Slade was right. If I didn't stand up to my father, he would never respect me enough to choose me to take his place. That was absolutely something he would be waiting for me to do.

"It wouldn't hurt to keep him waiting for a couple of minutes," I said slowly.

"Or longer." Slade looked at me meaningfully.

I licked my lips. "Fine. A few minutes, but he's going to be pissed off."

Slade smiled. "Good. No one ever made their dreams come true without stirring the pot and pissing a few people off. That's what makes people memorable. Not that anyone would dare to suggest you're forgettable."

"They better fucking not," I growled. I had no intention of being forgotten by anyone. That would be worse than being underestimated.

"Come on. Let's walk slowly to the front of the Academy." He let my wrist go and stepped back.

Having an intense conversation in the corridor

was one thing, flaunting the fact we were involved with each other, was another. The fact we were fucking was not a secret, but Brutham preferred we exercise some measure of discretion.

CHAPTER 23

LILA

My father was standing, leaning against his car when we stepped down the front steps of Brutham Academy. His arms were crossed over his broad chest, gaze watching us through half-lidded eyes. His expression was guarded. So much so I couldn't tell if he was pissed off or not.

He wasn't alone. I expected to see Chloe and maybe Zachary here. I didn't expect to see my half-sister, Kennedy Knight, or her three boyfriends.

I introduced them to Slade one by one. "Mannix Cassani, Ares Turner and Ice Miller. My sister Kennedy and my father, Samuel Bell. This is—" I raised my hand to gesture at Slade.

"Slade Lincoln," Dad finished for me. His eyes lingered on Slade. "You didn't think I'd do a thorough background check on everyone that works at Brutham Academy?"

"I wouldn't expect anything less." Slade shook hands with Dad, then offered his hand to Kennedy.

All three of her boyfriends stiffened.

"I wouldn't do that if I was you," Ice said with menacing pleasantness.

Mannix actually took a step forward.

Slade lowered his hand. "My apologies. I didn't mean to offend any of you." He was clearly not intimidated by their 'touch her and die' vibes.

"What are you doing here?" I directed the question at Kennedy. She was a couple of years older than me, with flaming red hair and freckles.

Beyond those, there was some family resemblance. Not as obvious as Chloe and I, but it was there. I'd noticed it the first time I met her, but I knew to look for it. At the time, she had no idea she was related to us. I felt a stab of remorse for taking her down to the basement, but at the time I was just glad it wasn't me going in there.

"I'm here to see how you are," Dad said. "Kennedy wanted to see Brutham. She happened to be visiting along with her boys."

Ares glared at him, apparently annoyed at being referred to as a boy.

Mannix didn't look too pleased either.

Ice went on smiling, like he always did. He looked sweet, but that was all a façade. He'd happily slice the skin off my body to see what I looked like underneath. I got the impression he'd love to get his hands on Chloe and me to compare the insides of a set of twins. To say he was slightly unhinged was an understatement.

Anyone with a drop of sense watched their backs when he was around.

"We came because Ric DiMarco is concerned he hasn't heard from Hunter or Parker," Mannix said coolly. He gave off an aura of not giving a shit about the twins. "Where are they?"

I frowned. "They went away on business for Reuben." Ric DiMarco answered to Caleb Brantley, who in turn answered to his brother, Reuben. Why come here instead of asking one of them?

Mannix scowled. He grabbed out his phone and stomped a few metres away before calling someone. I couldn't hear what he said, but his tone was respectful. Much more so than I ever got from him.

While Mannix spoke, Dad gripped my chin with his thumb and forefinger.

"How are you? I was worried when Chloe called me and told me what happened to you. It's out of character for you to get out of your sister's way. Especially as comprehensively as you would if you'd died."

"I wouldn't exactly have had a choice," I pointed out. "I didn't expect anyone to put toxic shit in a teddy bear."

His grip tightened to the point of pain. "You *should* have expected it. You should have anticipated that someone would try something. You let down your guard and you almost died because of it."

I stood still. Tears of pain gathered in the corners of my eyes.

"Chloe let Zachary give her a bear too," I whispered.

"This isn't about Chloe," he said firmly. "This is about you and what you did. You have to be more careful. Next time, you might not be so lucky." He loosened his grip and drew me in for a hug.

After a moment, I hugged him back. He wasn't wrong about anything, but the look of disappointment on his face was a stab straight into my heart.

"I'm sorry," I said softly. "I'll be more careful next time."

"Of course you will. You're a smart, resourceful young woman. You won't make any more mistakes."

"Yeah." No fucking pressure.

He stepped back as Mannix returned.

"I just spoke to Daisy Lasalle, she's unaware of

any assignment Reuben might have sent Hunter and Parker on. She's going to contact him and get back to me." He shoved his phone back into his pocket.

"Did you have them killed, Sam?" Ice asked cheerfully. "I'd be disappointed if you did and didn't let me take part." He glanced at me and his mask slipped slightly. He absolutely held a grudge against me and the twins for turning him and Kennedy in to Dad. If he had his way, I'd be hanging from chains in his workroom right now.

Slade caught his look and stiffened, moving over closer to me.

"Not yet," Dad said. "I did tell them to stay away from Lila."

"Maybe they finally took your advice and fucked off," Ares said with a grunt.

"Doubtful. They seemed to have attached themselves to my daughter." Dad gave me a dark look. I shouldn't be surprised he knew that. The walls had ears, particularly here at Brutham.

Only Kennedy seemed sympathetic. Of course she would, he didn't approve of her choice of boyfriends either. It seemed all of his daughters were destined to disappoint him when it came to our relationships.

"They've been very good to me," I said flatly. "All they want is to make me happy. If it wasn't for them,

I'd be dead. If they hadn't found me when they did—"

"If you hadn't accepted that teddy bear, none of that would have mattered," Dad said, straight to the point.

"Maybe you should take that up with your stepson." Slade clearly had enough with my father and his tone. "I haven't ruled out the possibility Chloe was involved in that too. Where are they anyway?" He gave me a look to remind me he'd suggested I not hurry out to see Dad. Evidently, neither had they.

"She's coming down the steps now." Ice nodded behind me. He gave her a smile that was more genuine than the one he gave me.

It seemed he'd taken sides. That was something I'd have to work on, or have him killed. I'd rather not do that. I might need Kennedy at some point in the future. Nothing would alienate her more quickly than killing one of her boyfriends. In the end, that was up to him.

"Dad." Chloe hugged him. Then she hugged Kennedy.

Our sister seemed as pleased to see her as Ice was. If Kennedy took sides against me too, then we may have a problem. If I had to deal with her, then I'd have to deal with all three of her boyfriends as well.

When had that headache started? My forehead throbbed.

Mannix's phone rang. He pulled it back out, glanced at the screen and took a few steps away again. He frowned as he listened and spoke to whoever was on the other end of the phone. The conversation lasted less than a minute. He stalked back over to us.

"Daisy Lasalle said Reuben knows nothing about where Hunter and Parker are. He didn't send them anywhere."

"What the fuck?" I stared at him. "Is she sure?"

He glared at me. "That's what she said Reuben told her. Either they don't know, or they don't see any reason for us to know. For what it's worth, she said Reuben sounded pissed off."

"Reuben always sounds pissed off," Dad said. "It's part of his asshole persona."

"Reuben would have good reason to sound pissed off if the twins went missing," Slade said.

"Oh, I don't know," Chloe said slowly. "It seems like that pair has caused him a lot of trouble recently. It wouldn't surprise me if he decided to deal with them." She looked all too fucking smug.

I wanted to scratch the expression off her face.

"They've never given him a reason to dispose of them," I said firmly.

231

"Are you sure about that?" Ice asked. "They've given a lot of people a lot of reasons to dispose of them. The list is long. Reuben, me, Mannix, Ares, Sam, his brother Zeke, that dude who plays keyboard for Wolf Venom."

"Penn," Kennedy said with a sigh.

Mannix actually growled. "Don't give me an excuse to have him killed."

She smiled adoringly and kissed his mouth. "You'd never kill the members of my favourite band. I'd never forgive you if you did."

He hooked an arm around her waist and pulled her hard against him. "You would forgive me if I had to paddle your ass until you do."

Dad cleared his throat. He turned cold, brown eyes to me.

"First you accept a present that almost kills you, then two of your...boyfriends go missing. I'm starting to think maybe Chloe—"

"I'm sure there's a reasonable explanation for whatever Hunter and Parker are doing," I said quickly. Surely he wasn't going to hold me responsible for events I had no control over?

Of course he would. Because I should have control over everything.

"They'll turn up in a couple of days with an explanation even you'll be impressed with," I added.

232

Dad snorted softly, clearly disbelieving.

In the corner of my eye, I saw Chloe looking even more smug. Would anyone mind if I strangled her with my bare hands right here?

Dad's gaze turned to Slade. "When I spoke to you a couple of days ago, you said the situation was under control."

I gaped. They knew each other?

Wait, when Slade was finger fucking me on his desk, was it was my *father* on the other end of the phone? He heard me groan. Fucking hell.

"It was," Slade said. "I didn't anticipate that Hunter and Parker weren't off doing a job for Reuben."

"What the fuck is going on?" I demanded.

"When I heard you were involved with Slade Lincoln, I contacted him," Dad said unapologetically. "I've used his services in the past."

I gave him a blank look.

"He's an assassin," Ice said louder than could possibly have been necessary.

I turned to Slade. He shrugged and nodded.

"It's true. I was trying to explain that, but it's not the kind of thing that comes up in regular conversation."

"The belt," I said slowly.

"Just the beginning of it, and one of many methods. This shouldn't change anything." He was telling me, not asking. Nothing in his expression suggested he thought I'd turn away from him because he was a hitman.

"It does, though," Ice said. "It makes you cooler than I thought you were."

"You're out of your fucking mind," Ares told him.

"Yeah, but not about this," Ice said. "If I didn't do forensic medicine, I would have become an assassin. I would have been good at it too."

"Yes, you would." Mannix patted him on the shoulder.

I rubbed my temples. This was all a lot to process.

Slade slipped an arm around me. "For what it's worth, I think your father approves of me."

Dad granted. "That might be a stretch, but I approve of you more than I approve of Hunter and Parker. If they don't turn up again—"

I was done with his bullshit. "If they don't turn up again, I'm going to be devastated. I know they can be trouble sometimes, but I care about them."

If I thought my words would sway him even slightly, I was wrong.

He waved dismissively. "I expect better from both of you. I don't know who got the better of who here, but I'm seriously considering the value of Zachary

taking over some day. Perhaps there are more important things than blood."

His words made me want to spill some.

Instead I lifted my chin. "You won't when I'm
finished. I'll show you who deserves to be head of the
Bell family."

I wished I felt as confident. Everything Dad said
had me doubting myself and wondering who the hell
I could trust. Including myself.

One more slip up and I could be totally fucked.

CHAPTER 24

HUNTER

"Any guesses on how many days have passed?" Parker asked.

"Same as the last time you asked me," I snapped. "I have no fucking idea. At least a couple."

Apart from Zachary and Chloe dropping in once in a while to throw us some food, literally, the hours blended into each other. Parker found a bucket in the corner, but that was starting to get full.

The smell was no fucking joke either.

I took a long, slow breath. "Sorry, bro. When I said we needed a vacation, this wasn't what I meant. It's getting to me a bit."

"Yeah, me too," Parker said softly. "I'd rather be paddleboarding on some island somewhere. Or jumping out of a plane."

"We can do those things when we get out of here,"

I promised. "You, me, Lila and Slade can run off somewhere. Stay away from all the bullshit for a while."

"You'd be bored in the first two hours," he pointed out.

"I'd last at least three," I protested. "All of them with my cock buried in Lila."

We'd tried to break the chains that kept us bound, but they were firmly attached to the wall. They wouldn't slide or break off our wrists, no matter how hard we tried. I'd even placed one against the wall and had Parker slam his foot against it over and over.

Unable to see well enough in the dark, he kicked me more than he kicked the fucking restraints. He tried, but in the end I had to tell him to stop. Keeping going was more dangerous than quitting.

I fucking hated quitting.

Once we realised all we could do was bide our time, I sat leaning against the wall, or trying to sleep. I couldn't think of anything but Lila and what was happening to her.

Did she know we were missing or had Chloe and Zachary spun some bullshit story to explain our absence? If they were doing anything to her... Touching her...

"You're grinding your teeth again," Parker said. "I'm just as pissed off about this as you are."

I unclenched my teeth. "I know you are. I just—"

Footsteps approached. The door creaked open. A light flashed directly in my eyes. The chain gave me just enough slack to raise my hand and shield them.

If one of the assholes got close enough, I could wrap it around their neck, but neither of them did. Maybe they were hoping we'd do that to each other. No such fucking luck assholes.

"Good news," Zachary said cheerfully. "You're getting out of here."

"It's about fucking time," I growled. "Undo these things and we'll be on our way."

I shook my wrist to rattle the chain. The first thing I was going to do was kill this asshole. I didn't even care if it was quick and painless, as long as it happened.

Zachary chuckled. "You misunderstand. You're leaving here, but we're taking you somewhere else. They finally figured out you're missing. If it took them this long to notice, I guess they didn't give a shit. We still don't want anyone nosing around looking for you."

"Funny, because that's exactly what I want," I said. "How about you fuck off and we'll sit here patiently and wait for them?" I lowered my hand and crossed my arms as best I could over my chest.

"We could leave you here." Chloe's voice came out

of the dark. "But the only thing they'd find is a matched set of dead bodies. Fortunately for you, you're still useful to us."

"If you think we're going to come quietly, you're wrong," Parker said.

"Parker is right," I said. "When we come, we do it loud enough that everyone knows."

"No one wants to think about you coming," Zachary said.

"I do," Parker said. "I'd much rather think about that than being stuck here."

"I'm starting to think we should have taken out their tongues the last time they were knocked out," Chloe said.

"We're glad you didn't; Lila likes our tongues," Parker said.

"Then shut the fuck and you might get to keep them," she snarled.

Parker glanced sidelong at me. "She's not very nice, is she? She pretends she is, but then when you get to know her, she's really not."

"I've noticed that," I said.

"Enough," she snapped. "Zachary, Dane."

I didn't realise Mr D was here too. I squinted at a dark shape in the shadows. He'd stayed back until now.

"Now we have a party," Parker said. He reeled

back as Zachary slammed his fist into his face. Parker's head bounced off the wall behind him. He let out a short cry of pain.

Dane grabbed his arm and held it while Zachary jabbed a syringe. He slid the needle into Parker's vein and depressed the plunger.

Parker tried to jerk away, but they held him down hard until his body sagged. They lowered him onto the floor where he lay still, his breathing shallow.

They rose and stepped over to me. Zachary pulled out another syringe.

"We can do this the hard way or the easy way," Dane said. His expression was ice cold, with a faint aura of triumph. He always was a motherfucker.

"I choose C, neither of the above," I replied lightly. "Also, I'm reporting you to the Board of Education, because I'm pretty sure there's laws against drugging your students."

He laughed. "There are also laws against killing teachers. Who do you think will get in more trouble?"

"The one doesn't have a rich family to bail him out." I gave him a smug smile.

He might have forgotten the DiMarco family was sorely lacking in power and influence these days. Exactly why he hooked up with Chloe in the first place. He was desperate to get back on top, literally and figuratively.

There was nothing worse than someone who was desperate as well as ambitious. If I was him, I would have gone crawling to Ric DiMarco. His cousin was having more success than he was. Whatever, I didn't really give a shit.

I didn't see Dane move until his fist landed on the side of my face. He connected so hard he drove me back with a grunt of pain. Only dropping my head at the last second stopped me from slamming it into the wall.

He drove his booted foot into my ribs a couple of times for good measure before grabbing my wrist and holding my arm out for Zachary.

Yeah, Dane was going to die after that. A bit of witty banter was one thing, punching and kicking a guy when he was chained up was another.

Zachary drove the needle into my vein. Before he pushed down the plunger he crouched with his mouth next to my ear.

"I just want you to know I'm having a lot of fun with Lila. She totally believes that I'm on her side now. She couldn't spread her legs fast enough for me. No wonder she didn't notice you were missing, she was too busy coming around my cock."

"You're a delusional prick," I spat. There was no way Lila would fuck that asshole. Would she? I didn't want to believe it, but if he somehow managed to convince her he was innocent, maybe charmed his way into her pussy as well.

"Maybe, but we have something in mind for her. She's going to love every minute of it." He chuckled.

"If you touch a hair on her head…" I slurred.

Several creative ways to kill him flashed through my mind before everything went dark.

Lila

I woke slowly. My thought were groggy, strained. My head ached like my brain was thumping against my skull. The headache that started when Dad was here, was worse now.

He, Kennedy and her boyfriends hadn't stayed much past that conversation. Slade had to go to some meeting.

What happened after that? I must have lain down for a nap. I didn't remember doing that. I also didn't remember my bed being so hard.

Beside me, someone groaned. A female groan.

What the fuck?

They protested, but I forced my eyes open. The light was dim. Barely enough to illuminate beyond a half a metre or so. Enough that I made out a small space, warmth pressed against me on three sides.

Not warmth, I realised. Bodies.

Breathing, whimpering, groaning, female bodies.

Panic started to rise. Where the hell was I?

On the fourth side of me was a wall. I managed to claw my way up until I was sitting.

The smell hit me. Sweat, urine and terror. How many of us were pressed into this small box?

The box was moving. The light in the gaps showed the world flashing by. We must be in the back of a truck.

"Where are they taking us?" I asked, hoping to get some kind of answer. Even as I said it, I knew.

One of the many pies my family had their finger in was human trafficking. It wasn't something I gave much thought to, until now.

Until I realised my sister found a way to sell me.

Hey, Lila here. Thank you for reading! Our story continues in Cruel. If you love a bonus scene in my point of view of my 'punishment' from Slade, you can get it here. Well, you can read it. I was the one who got it.

ABOUT THE AUTHOR

Maggie Alabaster writes reverse harem and, paranormal, sci-fi and fantasy romance.

She lives in NSW, Australia with one spouse, two daughters, one dog, and countless birds.

Jo Bradley writes contemporary romance.

Sign up for Maggie's newsletter! Sign Up!

Join Maggie's reader group! Join here!

Follow Maggie on Bookbub! Click here to follow me!

Check out Maggie's website- www.maggiealabaster.com

Sign up for Jo's newsletter

ALSO BY MAGGIE ALABASTER

Brutal Academy

Book 1 Heartless

Book 2 Cruel

Book 3 Vengeful

Court of Blood and Binding

Book 1 Song of Scent and Magic

Book 2 Crown of Mist and Heat

Book 3 Sword of Balm and Shadow

Book 4 Whisper of Frost and Flame

Dark Masque

Book 1 Bait

Book 2 Prey

Book 3 Trap

Saving Abbie

Book 1 Pitch

Book 2 Pound

Book 3 Session

Book 4 Muse

Book 5 Rhythm

Book 6 Encore

Novella Venomous

Saving Abbie books 1-4

Saving Abbie books 4-6 + Venomous

Ruthless Claws

Book 1 Ivory

Book 2 Crimson

Book 3 Elodie

Harmony's Magic

Book 1 Summoned by Fire

Book 2 Summoned by Fate

Book 3 Summoned by Desire

Shifter's Vault

Book 1 Discarded

Book 2 Deceived

Book 3 Disgraced

My Alien Mates

Book 1 Star Warriors

Book 2 Star Defenders

Book 3 Star Protectors

Academy of Modern Magic

Book 1 Digital Magic

Book 2 Virtual Magic

Book 3 Logical Magic

Complete Collection

Summer's Harem

Book 1: Shimmer

Book 2: Glimmer

Book 3: Flicker

Complete collection

Short reads

Taken by the Snowmen

Jingle All the Way

Also by Maggie Alabaster and Erin Yoshikawa

Caught by the Tide

Book 1–Pursued by Shadows

Book 2 Pursued by Darkness

Book 3 Pursued by Monsters